Basil is sick. He doesn't know what his illness is, but he knows he's slowly dying, which is the only reason he reached out to his estranged father.

Who manages to get himself killed before finding a way to heal Basil.

Lucian is on his way to visit his brother when he sees a man fall on the side of the road. He's stunned when that man turns out to be his mate. He just found his brother after thinking he was dead for most of his life, and now his mate, too?

Everything isn't okay once Basil and Lucian find each other, though. Basil is still sick, and not even the unicorn shifters of the Rosewood pack can help. He's running out of time, and that's one thing Lucian can't provide him with, no matter how much he wants to.

Just Right
Copyright © 2021 Catherine Lievens
ISBN: 978-1-4874-3139-6
Cover art by Angela Waters

Published by eXtasy Books Inc or
Devine Destinies, an imprint of eXtasy Books Inc

Look for us online at:
www.eXtasybooks.com or www.devinedestinies.com

JUST RIGHT
LEGENDARY SHIFTERS 5

BY

CATHERINE LIEVENS

CHAPTER ONE

Basil's head felt like it was about to explode. He did his best to act as if nothing was wrong and smiled at his mother. "I'm sure he'll be back soon."

His mom peeked out the window of their motel room. "He said he would be back a while ago." She turned to face Basil. "What if he changed his mind?"

It was a legitimate worry. Basil shared it, but he didn't want his mother to worry even more. "He told us he might have some trouble coming back. I'm sure it's only that."

"I hope you're right."

Basil reclined back onto the pillows on his bed. He hoped he was right, too. He didn't know what he would do if John didn't find a way to heal him.

He couldn't think of John as his father. John *wasn't* his father, except for the biological aspect. Basil had never even met him until he'd gotten sick and his mother had freaked out. Now they were in Springfield, waiting for a man who had cheated on his wife and had a child out of wedlock, hoping he'd find a way to heal Basil.

It was a disaster waiting to happen.

They didn't know what else to do, though. Basil and his mother had tried everything. They couldn't exactly go to normal doctors, since Basil's mom was a gorgon. Basil wasn't, but he was pretty sure he also wasn't merely human, especially since his father was a wolf shifter. Doctors would find out if they examined him, and who knew what would happen then. No, Basil's only hope was his father, and the man had disappeared.

He licked his dry lips. He was starting to wonder if they had to forget about John and focus on something else to try to heal him. Neither he nor his mother knew what was going on with him. Their only hope was supernatural healers, which was why Basil's mom had brought him to Springfield. She'd hoped his father's pack would be able to help, and John had promised they would once he'd found out about Basil, but he'd vanished.

Basil couldn't wait forever. He didn't know what his illness was, but he wasn't stupid. It was getting worse, which could only mean one thing. He didn't say it out loud because his mother was already worried enough as it was, but eventually, they were both going to have to face the likelihood that he might not make it.

He wasn't done fighting, though.

"He said he would come back," his mother murmured. She moved away from the window toward him. "We should have faith in him."

Basil snorted, and even that hurt. "I want to, but he's been gone for a while now. It's been days since the last time we heard from him, and it's obvious something happened to him. We can't just stay here and do nothing, not when he might never come back." And why would he? Basil was his son, but he'd never met him until Basil needed him.

Basil's mom had told him the story once he was old enough to understand. She hadn't known John was married when they met, and she'd been in love. But then she'd seen him in Springfield with his wife and she'd left, not wanting to confront him and have to listen to stupid excuses. She'd found out she was pregnant several weeks later, but she'd never gone back, and she hadn't let John know about Basil. Basil still wasn't sure how he felt about that, but he couldn't say he regretted not knowing John after finally talking to him.

Basil's mom sat on the edge of the mattress and wrapped her fingers around Basil's ankle, squeezing gently. "I know. What else can we do, though?"

"I should go to Rosewood."

Basil's mom shook her head. "You can't go there on your own. You heard what your father said. Rosewood and Springfield are at odds, and the Rosewood pack wouldn't take it well if John's son invaded their territory."

"John said the Rosewood pack doesn't like him, but it doesn't mean Rosewood is in the wrong."

"It also doesn't mean they're in the right. If you go, I need to go with you."

Basil knew that couldn't happen. His mother was a gorgon, and gorgons were extremely rare in the paranormal world. It would be too easy for the Rosewood pack to capture her, and Basil didn't want that on his conscience. He might not trust John entirely, and maybe he'd lied, but it was a risk they couldn't take. "I'll go on my own."

His mother's eyes narrowed. "You can't. You're too weak, and we don't have a car. Are you going to walk there? You need my help, Basil."

Unfortunately, she was right. Basil was ill, and that made it hard to move. His head was pounding, and his entire body hurt as if he were eighty instead of twenty-six. Still, he wouldn't put his mother in danger, not if he could avoid it. "You can't come, and you know why. I'll go on my own. I'm sure I can find a bus or something, and if I can't, Rosewood isn't that far. I promise I'll call."

"Like your father did?"

She had him there. "You know you can't trust him and that you can trust *me*. I wouldn't ignore you, not when I know you're freaking out."

She grimaced. "I know you wouldn't. I still can't let you go on your own, though. I don't trust your father. I know you'll call if you can, but what if you can't? We don't know anything about the Rosewood pack. Your father said—"

"He said a bloodthirsty alpha led the pack. I know. I was there. I don't trust him as far as I can throw him, though. We have no way to know whether or not he was telling the truth. I'm inclined to think he wasn't." Because if he was, Basil would die sooner than he expected.

He needed a healer. When his mother had contacted his father to tell him he had a son and that Basil was ill and no one knew how to help, he'd promised to find a unicorn shifter. It was Basil's best hope, which was the only reason Basil and his mother were here.

Basil had never wanted to meet his father. He didn't care about the man or the reason he'd cheated on his wife with Basil's mother. He wasn't looking for a father figure, only for a cure. The fact that his father had promised him one had made him hope, but now he was starting to realize he'd been right not to trust the man.

Basil pushed himself into a sitting position. "I have to go."

His mother looked like she was going to protest, but he was twenty-six. She couldn't forbid him anything. In the end, she just sighed heavily. "All right. But you have to call me. I can't just stay here knowing something might have happened to you. If you don't call, I'll come after you."

"Even if something does happen to me, you can't intervene. You know what would happen if you did."

"I'm letting you go on your own, but you can't expect me to stay back when my only son is in danger. If they're hurting you, I'm coming, and that's that."

Basil nodded. He knew when he was defeated, and this was one of those situations. "Fine. But don't come charging in too soon. Give me time to talk to the alpha and find out if he can help me."

"I'm giving you until tomorrow evening."

Basil supposed it was better than nothing. He would have the rest of today and the entirety of tomorrow to get to the Rosewood pack and explain what his problem was. He wasn't that far from Rosewood anyway. He only hoped his body would sustain him until he got there. "I promise. If you don't hear from me by tomorrow evening, you can come charging in." And she would. She would do anything to help him, including reaching out to a man who had betrayed her.

Basil did his best to hide how much he was hurting as he got ready. He had to take a break in the bathroom, and he suspected his mother knew what he was doing, but neither of them said anything about it. She desperately wanted to come with him, but they both knew it was safer for her if she stayed where she was. An alpha without scruples wouldn't hesitate to capture her and hold her prisoner to use her. There were so few gorgons, just like there were so few unicorn shifters. John had told them the Rosewood pack had captured two of them, and he'd been angry about it. Basil didn't trust John, but if the Rosewood pack really had two unicorn shifters, they might be able to help. Hopefully, the shifters weren't prisoners, but Basil only had one way to find out. He didn't care what John had said. The Rosewood pack might not be as bad as John tried to convince them, and there was only one way to find out.

Basil had to go there.

Once he was ready, his mother spent five minutes flitting around him. They were both nervous, but Basil had to go, and he did so after kissing her cheek and promising he would be back.

He hoped it wouldn't be a lie.

Lucian bopped his head to the sound of the music. He was smiling, and he couldn't stop.

He couldn't believe he'd found his brother. Owen had been lost to Lucian and his family for most of his life, and even though Lucian barely remembered him, having been only five when Owen had disappeared, he was eager to get to know his brother again.

Which was why he was headed to Rosewood to visit his brother and his brother's mate.

Owen wasn't what Lucian had expected, and neither was Lennox. He supposed he shouldn't be surprised. Lucian and his sister had grown up in a dire wolf pack, but Owen hadn't. He'd been adopted—or rather, kidnapped—into a wolf pack. Lucian still had a hard time understanding why the man who had abducted Owen had done so when he clearly hadn't cared about Owen. Once Owen's adoptive mother had died, his kidnapper had turned abusive. It was a miracle Owen had made it out of the Springfield pack, and an even bigger miracle that he'd found Lucian and the rest of the family.

Lucian knew his parents and grandparents wished Owen would move in with the dire wolf pack, but he understood why Owen didn't want to. It wasn't just that he'd met his mate and that they both lived in Rosewood, although that was probably a big part of it. It was also that he had no reason to trust the dire wolf pack. He'd gone through a lot, and he felt safe in Rosewood. That was enough for Lucian not to ask him when he planned to move.

Besides, it didn't matter. Even though Owen didn't live close to the dire wolf pack, they could travel back and forth, just like Lucian was doing. He and Owen had talked on the phone and texted often, and they'd decided that Lucian would visit for a week, maybe more. Lucian was excited. He was expected to become alpha after his grandfather and his mother—so not for a long time, thankfully—but he had no intention of doing that. He wasn't alpha material, and he should tell them about it.

He would, someday.

He didn't want to ruin their happiness, though. They'd just gotten Owen back, and eventually, the high from that would fade. Then Lucian would tell them he didn't want to be alpha. He knew they would understand and that they wouldn't force him into it, but they would still be disappointed. Some days, he was disappointed in himself. He realized it was stupid, though.

It started raining, and between that and the darkness, he had to focus on the road. It was his first visit to Rosewood, and he didn't want to have an accident or get lost. He was going to be late, but he still drove slowly. Owen would understand. What he *wouldn't* understand was if Lucian crashed his car because he was thinking about not wanting to be an alpha.

Lucian turned the music off so he wouldn't be distracted, and of course, his mom chose that moment to call him. He put the call on speaker. "I'm not there yet."

"Why not? You left a while ago."

"Because I'm not in a rush."

"You should be. You looked happy to see Owen. He's your brother."

Lucian couldn't help but smile. His mom had wanted to go with him, but he'd explained he wanted some time alone with his brother. They had to learn how to be together not just as a family, but also as siblings. Besides, he was pretty sure Owen was slightly uncomfortable with her and their father. It was harder for Owen to wrap his mind around the fact that he had loving parents than around the fact that he had siblings. Lucian hoped that eventually Owen would relax and welcome all of them into his life, but it would take time, and they were all aware of it. "I *am* eager to see him, but I doubt he'd be happy if I got myself killed in my rush to get to him."

Lucian's mom sucked in a breath. "Don't get yourself

killed. I just got one of my sons back. I don't want to lose the other one."

"I promise. I should probably hang up now, though. It's dark, and since you don't want me to get hurt, I need to keep my attention on the road."

"Call me when you're there. I want to make sure you're okay and to talk to Owen."

"I promise. I'm going to be a little late, so don't worry too much." Telling her that was pointless, but Lucian could try.

He realized he was going to be even later than he'd thought when he got a flat tire a few minutes after they'd hung up.

He guided the car toward the edge of the road, swearing. "Why did you have to do that now?" he asked out loud.

The car didn't answer. Lucian eyed the sky, but he couldn't see much except for the rain. It looked like he was going to have to get wet. He had an umbrella, but he doubted he could change the tire and hold it at the same time.

He did get wet. He'd never been good at changing tires and all that stuff, but he knew how to do it. Still, it took him much longer than he wished, and by the time he sat in his car again, he was dripping. He glared at the car and at the sky, then took his phone from the passenger seat to text his brother.

Got a flat tire.

It only took a few seconds for Owen to answer, as if he'd been waiting with his phone in his hand. *Do you need help?*

I already changed it, but please, have a towel ready when I arrive. I'm drenched, and I prefer my showers warm.

Owen's next text started with a sad emoji. *Will do. I hope you won't get a cold.*

I doubt I will, but thanks for worrying. I'm almost there.

I'll also get coffee ready. I'm sure you can do with something warm. You can get a shower and hot coffee as soon as you get here.

I don't know if I've already said it, but I love you.

Owen sent back a laughing emoji, and Lucian put his phone down. He started the car, then turned onto the road again. It should only take him another ten minutes to get there if he trusted his navigator, and he hoped it was correct. He needed out of these wet clothes.

Something moved at the corner of his vision, and he frowned. He squinted, trying to see what it was in the darkness. Hadn't Rosewood heard of streetlamps? He knew he'd seen something move, and hopefully, it was only an animal, but he doubted it. Whatever had moved was tall, which made him think it was a person.

If someone was walking along the side of the road in this weather and darkness, they had to be nuts. It was a recipe for disaster, and they were lucky they hadn't been hit by a car yet.

Sure enough, once Lucian's gaze stopped on a moving man, he realized he'd been right. It was a person.

The man was walking just off the road to Lucian's right. He was hunched over, no doubt trying to protect himself from the rain, and he wasn't dressed warmly enough for the weather. His jacket looked soaked.

What was the guy doing? It wasn't Lucian's business, but he wouldn't be able to forgive himself if something happened to this guy and he'd been able to do something about it. He might be about to pick up a serial killer, but he was a shifter. He could defend himself — probably. He had no way to know whether or not this guy was a shifter, too, but he had to go with the assumption he wasn't, or that if he was, he would be grateful and not try to kill Lucian. There was no way out of this, though. Lucian wasn't going to abandon the guy out there. He was walking on the edge of the road, which meant he didn't have a car and that he hadn't arrived wherever he was going yet.

Lucian slowed down the car, still peering at the guy. The guy stumbled. Was he drunk? That would make walking around in the dark an even worse idea, but at least it would make sense. If the guy was drunk, he probably hadn't thought much about what he was doing. He might not realize how dangerous it was for him to walk at the side of the road at night while it was raining. There was no way Lucian could abandon him. He slowed the car even more and guided it toward the edge of the road so he could stop.

Basil heard a car behind him and moved even further to the right. It was dark, and he prayed whoever was driving had seen him. It would be too easy not to in the darkness.

Maybe this wasn't such a good idea. He should have waited until tomorrow morning to leave the motel, especially since he didn't have a car. He'd needed to do something, though, and now, he was regretting it.

He was wet from the rain. He was in pain. He had no idea where he was or where he was going. The only thing he could do was continue walking and hope he'd eventually get to Rosewood.

Instead of passing by him, the car stopped. Basil tried to turn around to see what was happening, but he stumbled, and he knew he was going to fall before it happened. There was nothing he could do to stop it, so he let his body tumble on the ground.

It was cold and wet, and he shivered. He tried to get to his feet, but he couldn't. His body had used the last energy it had to get him here, and now, it refused to move. The cold had somewhat numbed the pain, so Basil supposed it wasn't all bad. Still, he knew what would happen if he couldn't get back up.

He regretted leaving his mother and that she probably would never know what had happened to him. There was nothing he could do but curl up, so that was what he did. It wasn't like this was unexpected. Both he and his mother knew that he would die eventually, and sooner rather than later.

She would know he had if he didn't come back, and while she would grieve, at least this would be over. It was better than not knowing what was going to happen to Basil. Still, he wished he could have said goodbye one last time.

He couldn't say he would regret dying, though. He'd been expecting it since he got sick and realized he wasn't going to get better. He'd hoped for a different outcome, and he didn't actually *want* to die, but he would be grateful for the end of the pain. It was one of the hardest things about this illness. The others were not knowing what was happening to his body and causing his mother so much pain.

It looked like all of that was over now.

He jerked when something warm touched his face. It took him a few seconds to realize it was hands, and when he did, he forced himself to open his eyes.

"I'm not going to hurt you. I'm trying to help," a man said.

Basil looked around. He couldn't see much of the man in the darkness, but he could still see the car. It had stopped close by, and it was obvious that this man had been driving it. Basil didn't understand why he'd stopped, although maybe it was because he'd seen Basil fall.

Not everyone was like Basil's father. Not everyone abandoned people in need.

"Are you drunk?" the man asked.

Basil blinked, not sure he understood the question. He opened his mouth to answer, but the only thing that came out was a croak.

The man frowned and reached down again. "Okay, whether or not you're drunk doesn't matter. I'm still going to help you. I'm going to carry you to the car. Don't start freaking out, please. Neither of us would be happy if I fell while holding you. I don't think you're in the right state to take more trauma than you've already had."

Basil doubted he would have the energy to freak out, but

11

he nodded slightly. He wasn't sure whether or not the man noticed, but since this man was going to help him either way, it didn't matter.

The man leaned down again and hooked his arms around Basil. He hauled him up, and Basil pressed himself closer to the man's chest. He was warm and smelled good, and Basil found himself relaxing almost immediately.

The man took a deep breath. "Shit."

Basil had no idea what was going on. He wanted to ask, but he didn't think he would be able to. He didn't even care. He was warm where his body touched the man's, and even though he was still getting wet because it was raining, he felt better than he had in a long time. His body still hurt, but his mind didn't. For whatever reason, he felt safe. He felt cared for. He knew this man wasn't going to abandon him on the side of the road, and that was all that mattered.

"What's your name?" the man asked.

Basil thought the man knew he couldn't speak, but he would try to answer, since he was asking. "Ba-Ba-Basil," he said. He was still freezing and trembling, and he tried to push himself even closer to the man.

The man sucked in a breath. "Basil?"

Basil nodded and buried his face against the man's neck. He smelled heavenly, and it made Basil wonder if maybe he'd already died. Was this heaven? He supposed he wouldn't be as cold as he was if that was the case, so maybe he was still alive.

The man cleared his throat. "Well, Basil, I'm Lucian. I'm going to carry you to the car and put you in the back seat."

"All right," Basil croaked.

"We can talk about everything else later, once you're dry and warm. You can explain why you were risking your life walking on the edge of the road."

Basil didn't want to explain. He wanted to bask in the

feeling of being home, even though he didn't understand it.

He never wanted to leave this man's arms. He didn't know why Lucian had stopped or why he'd taken pity on a stranger, but he wasn't going to protest. Even if Lucian was dangerous, even if he hurt Basil and killed him, it was nothing that wasn't already happening to Basil's body. It was reaching the end of what it could stand, and Basil was relieved.

He would soon be done with the pain, with the questions, with not knowing what was happening to him. He would be done with everything, and even though he was relieved, now that he'd met Lucian, he couldn't help but wonder what his life would have been if it had happened sooner.

He was never going to find out, but he supposed that was okay. At least he would have this one moment in which he could forget about his illness and everything else and focus on what being in Lucian's arms felt like.

Lucian had no idea what he was doing. He hadn't thought much beyond stopping and helping the man who had fallen and who, instead of getting back to his feet, had curled up and apparently waited to die. He hadn't expected Basil to do that.

He also hadn't expected Basil to be his mate.

There was no denying it. Even with the rain and the smell of gasoline coming from the road, he was sure of it. Basil was his mate, and something was wrong with him.

Lucian didn't know what to do, so he rushed to his car. He tried to be careful so they wouldn't tumble to the ground together. Whatever was wrong with his mate, he didn't want to make things worse. When he got to the car, he had a moment of hesitation. He needed to open the back door, but both his arms were around Basil. How was he supposed to do it without dropping him?

"I'm going to set you down to your feet," he told Basil.

Basil's eyes were closed, and Lucian wasn't sure he was listening to him or even that he was still conscious.

"Nod if you heard me. Please, Basil. I need to put you down so I can open the door. Once you're in the car, I have a blanket for you. I'll wrap it around you, and I'll head to my brother's house. He'll be able to help you." Or at least, Lucian hoped so.

Hopefully, whatever was wrong with Basil, it was only the flu or something like that. Lucian had never heard of a shifter getting the flu, but he supposed anything was possible, especially since he was getting mixed shifter scents from Basil. Two unicorn shifters lived in Rosewood, and they should be able to heal whatever was wrong with Basil.

Lucian's knees almost buckled in relief when Basil nodded against his throat. He leaned against the car and gently lowered Basil to his feet. Basil stumbled, but since Lucian had expected that, he hadn't entirely let go. He held Basil against his body with one arm while he opened the door with the other. Once that was done, he helped lower Basil to the back seat. "You can stretch out if you want. I don't care if you get the seat wet."

Basil blinked. Now that they were in the car, Lucian could see him better. He supposed he shouldn't be surprised that he found Basil attractive. If Basil was his mate—and Lucian was sure he was—it made sense that Lucian was attracted to him.

Basil's dark wet hair hung limply down his face, and Lucian pushed it aside to see his eyes. They were open, but only to slits. Even like this, he could see that Basil had dark eyes. His skin was pale, though, too much so. That probably had a lot to do with how cold Basil was to the touch, and it made Lucian freak out a bit more. "Stay here. I'll grab the blanket."

Basil didn't even react. Lucian had to stop freaking out, because he needed to get Basil to safety, and that wasn't going to happen if he couldn't think clearly.

He straightened and walked around the car, then opened the trunk and moved his bags around until he found the blanket he knew was there. Once he found it, he rushed back to Basil, but Basil hadn't moved. He lay slumped limply against the seat, either asleep or unconscious. Probably unconscious.

"Here you go," Lucian said. He spread the blanket on top of his mate and tucked it around him so it wouldn't slip off. "I'm going to go back to the driver seat and drive you to the Rosewood pack. It's where I was going before I found you and stopped."

Lucian was pretty sure Basil couldn't hear him, but he had to continue talking on the off chance that he could. He was a nervous talker, but more importantly, he didn't want Basil to freak out. He probably hadn't expected a stranger to pick him up, and Lucian wasn't sure Basil had realized they were mates. Even if he had, there was no way for him to know Lucian wouldn't hurt him.

Not that being mates meant Lucian wouldn't. He had no idea what he was doing, but he needed to do it fast.

He closed the door once he was sure Basil was settled in as well as he could, then walked around the car. Something caught his gaze, though, and he realized it was a backpack, probably Basil's. Lucian wasted a few moments rushing to it, then carrying it to the car. Basil was going to want it once he woke up.

Because he *was* going to wake up.

Once he was back in the car, Lucian drove as fast as he could without crashing the car. It was still raining, and he was even wetter than he'd been before, but he didn't care anymore.

He kept peeking at the back seat in the rearview mirror, but Basil wasn't moving. Lucian was pretty sure he saw him breathing, but he couldn't have sworn to it, and he was freaking out, even though he'd told himself he wouldn't. He couldn't lose his mate, not when he'd just found him. If Basil didn't want him, that would be fine. If he died, though, it wouldn't be.

When Lucian finally reached Rosewood, he sighed in relief. But he wasn't done yet—he still had to drive through the town to pack territory. He knew the Rosewood pack wasn't a big one, but he still had no idea where to go once he got there. He reached for his phone, quickly dialing Owen's number. "I need help," he said when Owen answered.

"You couldn't change the tire?"

It took Lucian a second to remember he'd had a flat tire. "I already did that, but I found a guy on the ground in the rain. He's my mate, and he's sick."

There was a moment of silence before Owen answered. "Where are you?"

"I found pack territory. I'm parking behind a house, but I don't know if it's yours. I'm going to get out of the car, grab Basil, and start walking. Please, come find me."

"I'm on my way."

Lucian didn't want to get Basil wetter and colder than he already was, but he felt he didn't have a lot of time. He turned the engine off, rushed out of the car, opened the back door, and reached for Basil. He sighed in relief when Basil murmured something and tucked himself against him the way he had earlier.

It wasn't easy to get Basil out of the car, but Lucian managed, and once he did, he hooked his arms around his mate again and hauled him up against his chest. Basil buried his face against Lucian's neck, and Lucian hoped it was a good sign. He wrapped the blanket around Basil as well as he could. It wouldn't be great protection against the rain and wind, but it was better than nothing.

He slammed the door shut with his foot, then he started walking around the house. There were other houses, arranged in a loose circle with a fire pit in the center. Most of the houses had a light on the porch, so it wasn't as dark as before. That also helped Lucian notice the men on one of the porches.

Lucian rushed toward them. At the same time, Owen and someone else—no doubt Lennox, Owen's mate—came toward him.

"We're almost there," Lucian murmured. "I'm sure my brother and his alpha will be able to help you."

"I'm dying," Basil mumbled.

"You're not. It's only a cold. I'm sure you'll be fine once we get you out of those wet clothes and warmed up."

"I'm dying," Basil repeated.

"What's going on?" Lennox asked.

Lucian's knees almost buckled in relief. "I'm not sure what's wrong with him, but I need help. *He* needs help." Lucian didn't care about anything else. He'd make sure Basil got everything he needed, even if he had to antagonize the Rosewood alpha—although hopefully, it wouldn't come to that.

CHAPTER TWO

When Basil woke up, he was warm and comfortable. He waited for the pain to hit. It always did, but especially so in the morning.

He didn't know where he was. The motel bed he'd been sleeping in recently wasn't as comfortable as the one he was in now, so he wasn't there, but he found that he didn't care. Maybe he was dead. Maybe that was why he wasn't in pain and he felt so good. If this was what death was like, it wouldn't be so bad, except for the fact that he'd lost his mom. He would miss her.

It couldn't be heaven, though. He had to go to the bathroom, and his body was letting him know that he didn't have a lot of time to make that happen. The last thing he wanted was to soil himself and this comfortable bed, so he groaned and opened his eyes.

He blinked. He'd never seen the room he was in. Now that he was a bit more awake, he realized he wasn't dead.

Where was he, though?

The room was a normal bedroom. There was the bed he was in, a nightstand right next to it, and a dresser in front of it. The door next to the dresser was cracked open, and Basil saw it led to a bathroom. The other door was closed, and he suspected it led to the rest of the house. The walls were a light gray, the furniture wooden, and it gave Basil the sense of being home, even though he wasn't.

There was also a chair next to his bed and a man sleeping in it. His upper body was pressed against the bed, his face buried into his crossed arms. The only thing Basil could see was a mop of dark hair, and he found himself reaching out to touch it. His fingers barely made contact, but it was enough for the man to jerk into a sitting position.

Lucian. Basil remembered now.

Lucian had found Basil on the side of the road when he had fallen. He'd carried him to his car, and he'd taken care of him. That was all Basil could remember, unfortunately.

Lucian's gaze moved to Basil, and his eyes widened. "You're awake," he said.

Basil smiled. He was still waiting for the pain to hit, and he could feel it coming. His body was tingly, and not in a good way. Still, he hoped he had a few minutes so he could introduce himself and talk to Lucian without feeling like an idiot. "I don't know where I am, though."

"In Rosewood pack territory. Don't you remember what I told you yesterday?"

Basil shook his head. "I barely remembered you until just now." He bit his lower lip. "I have a few questions, but I need to use the bathroom first." Before his bladder exploded.

Lucian's eyes went even wider, and he scrambled to his feet. "Of course! Do you need help? The bathroom is just there, but I can go with you if you need me to."

Basil hesitated. "I'd like to try alone, if that's okay?"

"Of course it's okay. Just give me a shout if you need help. I'm going to be right here."

Basil nodded and pushed the comforter away. It was warm and soft, and he couldn't wait to bury himself in it again. He swung his feet to the floor, wincing when he felt how cold it was on his bare feet. He swayed as soon as he was in an upright position, and he had to reach out and hold himself up against the wall, but he didn't fall. Lucian didn't try to catch him, either, and he didn't say anything about it. Basil was grateful for that—and relieved.

He was weak. He knew he was. He didn't need anyone to remind him of it or to try to coddle him.

He shuffled his way to the bathroom, relaxing once the door was closed behind him. He couldn't hide what was happening from Lucian, even though he wished he could. He didn't know why appearing strong was so important to him when it came to Lucian, and he didn't have the mental energy to investigate it, but he wanted it. It wouldn't happen, though, so he went through the motions as fast as he could without falling on his face, using the toilet, then washing his face and hands. He eyed the shower, wishing he could take one but knowing he would probably faint if he did so. He had the last time. He didn't want to risk it right now, so instead of stripping, he turned to the door that would lead him back to the bedroom.

Lucian was still there, just like he had promised. He stayed in the chair as he watched Basil walk to the bed, but when Basil tripped on the carpet, he was suddenly by his side, holding him up and making sure he didn't fall on his face.

Basil didn't want to appear weak, but he was grateful for Lucian's presence. Falling would have been more painful than having his lack of strength exposed, especially since Lucian already knew something was wrong with him.

Lucian helped Basil into the bed again, and once he was on his back, he even tucked the comforter around him. Basil closed his eyes and took a deep breath, only for his eyes to fly open again in shock. "What's that smell?" he asked.

Lucian straightened and rubbed the back of his neck, sheepish. "That would be me. I was wondering why you weren't saying anything, but now I realize that you didn't notice."

Basil tried to get into a sitting position, but Lucian was having none of that. He gently pushed Basil back to the mattress, smiling at him. "Stay there. I need to call the healer."

"I want answers first. What did you mean?" Basil's heart raced. It couldn't be. He couldn't have met his mate just as he was about to die.

"I realized yesterday. You snuggled against me when I carried you to the car, and I smelled you. I knew you were my mate then, but I wasn't sure you had noticed. Now, I know you hadn't."

Basil slowly nodded. He had now, and he didn't know what to do with the information. He closed his eyes, needing a few moments.

This wasn't possible. He'd never been one to yearn to meet his mate, although he wished his mother had met hers. Now that he was going to die, she would be alone, and there was nothing he could do about it.

Why was fate so cruel to him and Lucian? Why had they met now, when Basil was going to die and Lucian would lose him before even having him?

None of it made sense, but Basil couldn't deny what he was smelling. Lucian was his mate. There was no ignoring that, and now, Basil was going to have to wrap his mind around it and make a decision.

If he was selfish, he would want to be with Lucian — and he did want that. He didn't know how long he still had, but spending this time with his mate, being loved and cared for, would be good. It wouldn't be for Lucian, though. It would give him a chance to fall in love with Basil, and when Basil died, Lucian would be alone again. It wasn't fair to him, but Basil didn't know if he had it in him to stay away from his mate.

He wasn't that strong. All his strength was going to fighting the disease that was slowly killing him, and he didn't know if he had the strength to stay away from Lucian. He didn't know if he could make that decision. Lucian would want to know why Basil didn't want him, and Basil didn't want to hide it from him. It might be easier, but it wouldn't be fair.

Lucian cleared his throat. "I'm going to call the healer and the alpha. They both wanted to see you when you woke up, and now, you have."

Basil nodded. "Thank you."

"I know it's a shock for you, and I'll understand if you don't want anything to do with me. Just, please, take a moment to think about it, okay? You're not feeling well, and you might make a decision you'll regret."

Basil was pretty sure he would regret anything that happened at this point, but what was he supposed to do? He couldn't deny Lucian was his mate, which meant he had to deal with it. He wasn't sure he was strong enough, but the only alternative was ignoring it, and that wasn't something he could do.

Lucian didn't know what to make of Basil's reaction to the knowledge they were mates, but he did his best not to obsess over it. Basil was hurt. He'd gone through a lot, apparently, and he had to recuperate. The last thing he needed was for Lucian to push him to make a decision about this. Besides, even if Basil weren't sick, it would be too soon. They didn't know each other, and even though they were mates, they didn't owe anything to the other.

He left the bedroom, wondering what was next. The healer had been worried when she'd examined Basil, and even the unicorn brothers hadn't seemed happy about whatever was going on with him. It made Lucian worry even more, but since there was nothing he could do about it, he headed to the kitchen.

Everyone was gathered there. There was Camden, the Rosewood alpha, and his mate, Toby. Toby was one of the unicorn shifters, as was his brother, Sam. Sam was sitting in front of him, one of his boyfriends on each side of him. Owen and Lennox were there, too, and they all looked up when they heard Lucian.

Lucian forced himself to smile even though he didn't feel like it. "He's awake."

Sam shot to his feet. "I'm going to call Naila. She'll want to know."

"I told him the healer would want to see him. He went to the bathroom, but he's back in bed."

"You should go back to him. We'll be right there." Sam's expression softened. "We can't make any promises, but we'll do our best."

Lucian raked a hand through his hair, his fingers catching in a tangle. "It would make me feel better if you told me what was going on."

"We can't. I know you're Basil's mate, but we can't tell you what's happening with him if he's not okay with it. I'm sorry."

"I understand." Lucian truly did. Sam was right. He and Basil were mates, but they'd just met. Basil might not want anything to do with Lucian, and if that was the case, he would disappear from Lucian's life as quickly as he'd appeared in it.

Lucian's gaze caught Owen's. Owen smiled at him, but the smile was full of pity and worry. Lucian knew his brother was worried about him more than Basil, but luckily, he didn't ask Lucian how he was. Lucian wasn't sure he had an answer to that. "I'm going back to him," he explained. "I'll see you later?"

"Of course. I'm not going anywhere. I'm here for you, and so is Lennox."

Lucian looked at Lennox, who nodded. He was silent, but then, he always was. Owen did a lot of talking for both of them, and Lennox seemed perfectly okay with it.

Lucian turned around and left the kitchen. He should have asked whether or not he could bring Basil something to eat, but he supposed the healers would want to see him first.

He didn't know what Basil wanted, but until he told him to stay away, Lucian would stick by his side and take care of him. It was the only thing he could do, and he would do it unless told otherwise.

He gently knocked on the door before opening it. Basil was still in bed, but he rolled his head to look at Lucian.

"I was wondering if you'd come back," he said.

"I just went to the kitchen to talk to the alpha and the healers. They'll be right here."

Basil looked away, biting his lower lip. "Will the alpha kick me out?"

Lucian frowned. "Why should Camden kick you out?"

Basil sighed. "It's a long story."

"I suppose we're all going to find out soon enough. Do you need anything? I can get you food or something to drink. Or I can help you to the bathroom again if you need to wash up."

"Or you could give him space to breathe," Owen said behind Lucian.

Lucian turned around and glared at his brother. "I'm not overbearing." He frowned and turned to Basil again. "Am I?"

Basil shook his head. "You're not. I promise."

"You'd tell me if I am, right?" Lucian didn't want Basil to run, but he wasn't sure how to make sure he didn't.

He'd had relationships in the past, even had a few serious ones. None would be as serious as the relationship he would have with his mate, though.

That was, if he and Basil ever had a relationship.

Lucian couldn't be sure, and it drove him crazy. He wanted to claim Basil in the most basic sense of the word. He wanted to make Basil his, to make sure everyone knew they belonged together. It was instinct, an instinct Lucian couldn't follow for now, and he had to swallow and bite the inside of his cheek not to reach for Basil.

"I can go if you need me to," he said slowly.

Basil shook his head and tried to sit up again.

Since he clearly wasn't going to stay on his back, Lucian rushed to his side and helped him settle against the pillows.

"I want you to stay," Basil said. "You're my mate, and you deserve to know what's going on."

"You're sick, aren't you?"

Basil looked away, but he nodded. "I am. I need a unicorn."

Someone knocked on the open door. Owen answered and stepped out — which meant it was probably Lennox — leaving Basil and Lucian alone again. Since Basil wanted Lucian to stay, Lucian went to sit in his chair again. He hovered there, on the edge of the chair in case he needed to spring into action to help Basil.

"I made it to the Rosewood pack, then?" Basil asked.

"You did. This was where you were heading?"

"It was. I heard that the pack has two unicorn shifters, and they're my last chance."

Lucian grimaced. "I want to ask, but you said you wanted to tell everyone at once."

"It will be easier."

Lucian looked at Basil. He was still gorgeous, and thankfully, he wasn't as pale as he'd been last night. Still, he looked weak, and it was obvious something was wrong with him. He was too thin, and there were deep shadows under his eyes, as if he hadn't slept in a week. His hands trembled when he pulled the comforter higher on his body, as if he was cold. Maybe he was, even though the room wasn't.

"Do you need anything? I can bring you whatever you feel like, food or drink, more blankets, anything," Lucian offered. He needed to do something to help his mate, but he didn't know what.

"I don't need anything, but thank you," Basil murmured.

Lucian flopped against the back of the chair. "I'm too much, aren't I? You can tell me if I'm too fussy. I won't be offended."

Basil smiled. "You're not. All my life, I've only had my mother take care of me. This feels nice." He swallowed heavily. "Even though I should probably stop it."

Lucian frowned. "Why? You're my mate. It's normal for me to take care of you. And if you think I'm going to demand something from you in exchange, I'm not. I would take care of anyone in this situation, and the fact that you're my mate doesn't change anything."

Basil blinked. "But you have to admit you're especially fussy because I'm your mate."

Lucian shrugged. "Maybe. What does it change, though? You're special to me, but it doesn't mean we have to be together. You're free to go anytime you want, Basil."

Basil snorted. "I'm not going anywhere. This is where I had to go, and now that I'm here, I'm hoping to get help."

"I hope you can get help, too." Because the thought of the pack not being able to help him sent Lucian into a panic.

Basil was sick. That much was obvious, and from the way Sam and Toby had been acting, Lucian knew it was bad. They were unicorn shifters, and if they couldn't heal Basil with their gift, something was very wrong. Lucian didn't know what yet, and he wasn't looking forward to finding out. He knew fear, but this was an entirely new kind of terror.

Basil wanted to say more, but he didn't know what. He wanted to reassure Lucian, and he couldn't. Instead, he asked, "Who's that guy who came in earlier and told you to give me space?"

That brought the smile back to Lucian's face. "That would

be Owen, my brother."

"I should have known. You look like each other."

"We do? I guess it's hard to see for me. We didn't know Owen was still alive until a few weeks ago."

Basil had no idea what Lucian meant by that. "Do you want to tell me?"

"I think you should rest. Camden and the healers will be here soon."

"And I'd like to think about something else for a bit. Please?" Basil didn't like begging, but he wasn't beyond it to keep Lucian close. "Unless you're uncomfortable. You can go, if you don't want to stay. I know you said you don't expect anything from me just because we're mates, but the same goes for you. You don't have to stick around if you don't want to. We might be mates, but we just met." And Basil was still so confused.

He wanted a happy life with Lucian. He wanted them to date, to get to know each other, and to fall in love.

He wouldn't have time for any of that.

It wouldn't be fair to Lucian to rush into it. It wouldn't be fair for Lucian not to know that Basil was dying. He might suspect something was wrong, but he didn't know what, and he would be shocked when he found out. Basil didn't want to tell him, but he had to. It was one of the reasons he wanted to wait, though. If he had to tell his story, he wanted to tell it once and be done with it. He didn't know if the Rosewood pack alpha would kick him out or allow his unicorn shifters to help him, but either way, Lucian would know, and Basil would, too. He would know if he had to find another way to be healed, or rather, if he should make his peace with death. He'd know what Lucian was planning on doing either way.

"It's a long story," Lucian said as he settled back against the chair. "My brother and I are dire wolf shifters."

"Aren't those prehistoric wolves?"

"They are. We're extremely rare, and we've been hiding, very much like unicorn shifters. Anyway, about twenty-five years ago, our pack passed through these territories. It wasn't a big pack, just my parents, my grandparents, and me and my siblings, including Owen. He was only a year old back then, and during the night, he snuck away. He disappeared, and we never knew what happened to him, not until recently."

"You found him again?"

"He found us. We had no idea he was alive."

"How did he do it? What happened to him back when he disappeared?"

"He was kidnapped. A man from a nearby pack, the Springfield pack, took him from our family. His wife wanted a child, but she had trouble carrying a pregnancy."

Basil was horrified. "So that man took Owen from you to give her a child?"

Lucian nodded. "Exactly. They raised Owen, never telling him where he came from. He only knew he was adopted, and since he was forbidden to shift by his father, he didn't even know he was a dire wolf. He believed he was a monster all his life, until he met Lennox, his mate. Lennox convinced him to shift, and they found out that Owen was a dire wolf. Camden knew about our pack, so he contacted us."

The story was incredible. It made Basil wishful. He couldn't help but wonder if he had a family out there somewhere, too, even though he knew that wasn't the case.

His mother didn't have a family. That was why she'd gone to Basil's father when he'd gotten sick. She didn't have anyone else to turn to, and she would do anything she could to make sure Basil was okay. John hadn't been able to help, though. He probably still hadn't contacted Basil's mother, and the thought made Basil's stomach churn.

John was his father. He might not have raised Basil, but nothing would change that fact. If he didn't care about Basil even though he'd helped bring him into this world, who would? Basil had no idea if John was still married, if he had other children, maybe parents and siblings. Even if that was the case, though, he doubted John would want any of them to meet him. He'd been clear — he wanted Basil to wait at the motel and let him handle everything. Basil wasn't to go to the John's pack and ask about him or tell anyone who he was.

And Basil had obeyed. He didn't care if his father was ashamed of him or wanted to keep him a secret, as long as he found a way to heal him.

"Are you okay?" Lucian asked.

Basil forced himself to smile. He didn't want Lucian to worry. He was doing enough of that for both of them. He was pretty sure Lucian would worry regardless, but they could act as if nothing bad was happening for a bit.

"What happened to the man who kidnapped Owen?" Basil asked. Lucian had mentioned the Springfield pack, which was the pack John belonged to. Basil wasn't surprised to find out that it wasn't a good pack. If the members were like his father, well, he didn't want to meet any of them.

"John was executed a few days ago. It wasn't just that he kidnapped a baby from his family, but also that he took Toby, Camden's mate. He kidnapped an alpha mate, and he had to pay for that."

Basil felt like he was going to throw up. "John?" His voice shook, and he hoped Lucian wouldn't notice. It had to be a coincidence. Right?

Lucian frowned. "That was his name, yes."

"When was he executed?"

The door opened before Lucian could answer. Lucian started to rise, but Basil grabbed one of his hands. He couldn't face this alone.

Now he knew why John hadn't come back. He was dead. He was *never* coming back, and he was never helping Basil.

29

No matter how much Basil wanted to believe it was a coincidence, he knew it wasn't.

A tall man stepped into the room. He wasn't alone. An entire group of people came in after him. The first man had to be the alpha, but Basil had no idea who the others—two guys who looked like each other and an older woman—were.

Basil bit his lower lip. He'd just found out that his father had been a horrible man, and now, he was afraid. He couldn't hide this from the pack, and he didn't want the alpha to kick him out just because of who his father was. He couldn't change it, and he hadn't had a say in that decision.

The first man smiled softly. "It's good to see you awake. My name is Camden, and I'm the Rosewood pack alpha."

Basil was glad he was in a sitting position rather than flat on his back. "My name is Basil."

"Lucian told us. Are you feeling up to talking now? If not, the healer is here, and she can help you."

Basil turned his attention to the older woman. She smiled at him, too. It was overwhelming, and it made Basil feel guilty but also comforted.

"My name is Naila. I gave you a painkiller, and I hope it's working."

Basil couldn't help smiling back. "It is. I haven't felt this good in a long time. Thank you." The pain would be back sooner rather than later, but for now, he was okay.

She nodded, but she looked worried. "I want to examine you again, but I think that both I as well as Sam and Toby would like to know what happened to you first. It might help us understand better what's going on with you."

Basil sighed. "Of course. I'll explain everything I can." He hesitated and turned his attention back to Camden. "I'm on foot. If you kick me out, I'm not sure I could actually leave, not in the state I'm in."

Camden frowned. "Why would I kick you out?"

Basil didn't want to explain, but he had to. "You might want to once you find out that I'm John's son."

The frown on Camden's face deepened. "John?"

Basil swallowed. "From the Springfield pack. Apparently, he kidnapped Owen and your mate."

Lucian didn't know what to say. How could his mate be John's son? "But John kidnapped Owen because he and his wife couldn't have children," he pointed out.

Basil wasn't looking at any of them when he answered, but rather keeping his focus on his free hand. "I wasn't born to his wife. He had an affair with my mother. She had no idea he was married, and when she found out, she left. She didn't know she was pregnant with me back then, and when she realized, she decided to stay away."

"Why don't you start from the beginning?" Camden asked.

Basil looked at him. "You're not kicking me out?"

"I don't see why I should."

"My father took your mate."

"He did. *You* didn't, though. I won't have you pay for something your father did. I don't know what to think yet, and I probably won't until I know the entire situation. So please. I'm listening, and so is everyone else."

Basil was still holding Lucian's hand, and Lucian squeezed. He was in shock, but he didn't want his mate to think he was angry at him. Basil couldn't do anything about who his father was, and from the sound of it, he wasn't happy about it.

Basil smiled gratefully and looked at Camden. "There's not much to say. John was my father, and he took your mate. No one would blame you for deciding not to help me."

"Just tell me."

"All right. Well, my mother stayed away from my father

for decades. I'm twenty-six, and while she was always honest with me about who my father was and why he wasn't in my life, she never actually told me much about him. I didn't want to know, either. As far as I was concerned, he hurt my mother, and he'd cheated on his wife. He wasn't someone I wanted to meet."

"But something changed," Camden gently prodded when Basil didn't continue.

"Something did. I started getting sick. At first, it was only headaches and exhaustion. None of the medicines I took helped. I saw a few healers, but they couldn't do anything. The pain spread to my entire body, and I feel like I'm being torn apart most days. I've been getting weaker, and I can barely sleep or eat. It's too painful. My mother didn't know how to help me, and she decided to contact John. He was the only person she could reach out to. We came here and met him."

Basil looked at Toby and Sam, who were still hovering behind Camden. "I'm sorry. John agreed to help me. I still don't know why, since he didn't even know about me before that day. He told us he would find a unicorn shifter. I suspect that's why he kidnapped you."

Toby nodded. "It makes sense. He wanted me to heal someone, but he never said who or what was going on. He should have called Camden and talked to him instead of taking me. I would have helped then." He paused and frowned. "I'm still going to help, if I can. I don't care who your father was."

"Thank you. You have to know everything before you agree to help me, though."

"You still haven't told us everything?"

Basil shook his head. "It's nothing bad. Well, maybe not. How are the two of you treated here?"

Lucian frowned. That question had come from out of

nowhere, and he wasn't sure he understood.

"What do you mean?" Toby asked.

"You're a unicorn shifter, and so is your brother. Are you prisoners? Are you being forced to stay here and heal people?"

Lucian snapped his attention to Camden. The alpha didn't look offended, though. He was frowning, but he wasn't kicking Basil out, which was good.

"We're not," Toby said gently. "Camden is my mate, and my brother found his mate in the pack, too. We *would* be allowed to leave if we wanted to, though. We just don't. We're happy here. I won't say it's not complicated, because some packs aren't happy that the Rosewood pack has two unicorn shifters, but we're dealing with it. Is that what the problem is? Are you a rare shifter?"

"I'm not."

Lucian squeezed Basil's hand again. He wished he could do more, especially when he heard the pain in Basil's voice. There wasn't, though. The only thing he could do was be there for his mate, but he didn't feel like enough.

"My father was a wolf shifter, as I'm sure you know. My mother isn't, though. She's a gorgon."

Lucian sucked in a breath. "That's not possible," he murmured. He knew about gorgons. He'd always been interested in rare shifters, maybe because he was one himself. Gorgons weren't shifters in the sense that they could become an animal, but they did have a shifted form that included serpentine hair, boar tusks, and wings. More importantly, in this situation, gorgons were always female. They only bore daughters.

Basil smiled at him. "I see you understand what's weird about the situation."

"Not everyone does," Toby grumped. "Maybe you could explain?"

"Gorgons are extremely rare, possibly even more than

unicorn shifters. They're all women. All the children they have are daughters."

"But you're a man."

Basil nodded. "My mother was stunned when she had a boy. She tried to find out what it meant, but no one knows. No one knows why I can't shift into a wolf or why I don't have a gorgon form, either. I should be able to shift either way, but I've never managed. I'm neither gorgon nor wolf shifter." He sighed heavily. "And now that John is gone, I don't know if I'm going to be able to find help."

"My pack and I will do everything we can to help you," Lucian declared. He should probably talk to his mother and grandfather first, but he knew they would help. They would even if Basil weren't his mate, but he was. It would be important to them.

"We'll help, too," Camden said.

"Even though my father hurt you so much?" Basil asked him.

"Again, you're not your father. Unless you plotted with him to kidnap Toby?"

Basil looked horrified. "I didn't. I would never hurt anyone."

"Even if it's to save your life?"

"Even then. I might not know what's happening to me, but it hasn't changed who I am. I wouldn't want someone to be hurt so that I can be better. I've been dealing with this illness, whatever it is, for a while now. I've accepted the fact that I might not make it."

Lucian had to swallow hard. He'd just found Basil. Surely he couldn't lose him already?

"We'll do everything we can to make sure that doesn't happen," Naila said. She didn't look certain, though, and Lucian's stomach churned.

"But?" Basil asked.

Naila sighed. "But Toby and Sam and I examined you when you were unconscious. We have no idea what's going on with you. I tried to help with the painkiller, and I can give you more, but it's not helping with the illness. It's making you feel better, which is good, but I think that it's the only thing I can do for you."

"We'll continue trying," Toby said. "And hopefully, now that you have a way to manage the pain, you'll be able to get more rest and eat. It's going to be important. We need you to be at your best if we want a chance to heal you."

Basil's hold on Lucian's hand tightened. "I don't know what to say. Thank you. When John didn't come back to tell us what had happened, I thought it was over for me. I can't believe you're helping me anyway."

"Is that why you were on the road on your own?" Lucian asked. "You said you were coming here. Were you going to beg for help?"

Basil nodded. "I didn't know what John did to the Rosewood pack. He said you guys were keeping two unicorn shifters prisoners and that it wasn't fair. I had no idea what he was planning or that he was lying. When he didn't come back, I knew something had happened to him, or at the very least, that he didn't care about me. This was the only thing I could do."

"You were in pain, yet you decided to walk here."

"I had no alternative." Basil straightened. "I have to call my mother. I promised her I would, and she's going to freak out if she doesn't know I'm okay. Then she'll come here. And trust me when I say that no one wants that to happen."

"Is she going to be a problem for the pack?" Camden asked.

"She's not dangerous, if that's what you're asking. But she's worried about me. She's scared. I'm her only child, and she doesn't have anyone else."

"Not even other gorgons?"

Basil shook his head. "She was never close to any of them, but they shunned her when they found out she had a baby boy. We only have each other, and she's been next to me every step of the way since I got sick."

Camden nodded. "I understand. Well, feel free to call her and to tell her to come here. She can stay with us while we try to find out what's going on with you."

Lucian relaxed. He'd already known Camden wouldn't kick Basil out, not as long as Basil didn't have anything to do with Toby's kidnapping. There was no way to know what would happen next, but at least now, Basil would have a chance. Lucian didn't know how he felt about any of this, but it would be too easy to give in to despair at the thought that his mate was ill and might die.

For now, he was going to focus on Basil and make sure he was as happy and comfortable as possible. Everything else, including Lucian's feelings, could come later.

CHAPTER THREE

Basil was feeling better, but he knew it didn't mean any-thing. It certainly didn't mean that he was healed and that he'd be able to skip into the sunset with Lucian as if every-thing was perfectly fine.

Everything was *not* perfect.

Basil had managed to find not one but two unicorn shifters, but he was still sick. He supposed he should be grateful for the painkillers Naila concocted for him, since it made it pos-sible to have a decent life, but it wasn't what he wanted. It wasn't a cure, and he knew that eventually, they would stop working, and he would die.

He'd never actually wanted to die. He'd wished it would happen a few times when the pain had been so strong that he could think of nothing else, but it had been a fleeting thought. Basil wanted to live, especially now that he'd met Lucian.

"Are you sure you don't need anything?"

Basil blinked at his mother. She'd been fussing over him, just like she always did, and he'd tuned her out. He seemed to have more trouble focusing lately, and it was worrying. "I'm fine."

She frowned. "You're not. I thought the Rosewood pack would be able to help."

"They're trying."

His mom pressed her lips together and squeezed his hand. "It's not enough."

It wasn't, but Basil didn't blame anyone. How could he? Sam and Toby, along with Naila, were doing their best to heal him, but they didn't even know what the problem was. Basil was weak and in pain, but those symptoms could point to any illness, and without more details, it was next to impossible to understand what was happening to him. They weren't sure they could heal whatever he had since unicorns were specialized in wounds and broken bones.

They were still trying, and it was heartbreaking to watch them every time they realized that nothing they'd done had helped.

Basil plastered a smile on his face and focused on his mom. "I'll be okay. We just have to find out what's going on. Once we do, they'll be able to do something."

She pursed her lips. "We don't have that much time."

She was right, but Basil was going to ignore it. "We have enough. Why don't you go to the kitchen to get yourself something to eat? And maybe have a nap later? You've been taking care of me for a long time, but now you have help. You don't have to be by my side twenty-four-seven."

"How can I rest when my only child is dying?"

Basil sighed. "I don't know, but worrying and hovering isn't going to help. I know you're tired, Mom. I'm not going anywhere, and for now, I'm feeling okay. Lucian will keep an eye on me if you're afraid something will happen, but I'm sure I'll be fine."

Luckily for Basil, Lucian wasn't as overbearing as his mother. It probably was because he hadn't seen Basil the way his mother had. She'd been right next to him ever since he'd gotten sick, and she knew how bad it could get. Lucian didn't, and Basil was pretty sure he would freak out if he found out.

Hopefully, he wouldn't.

Someone knocked on the bedroom door. Basil and his mom looked at each other, and after one last smile and a kiss on the forehead, she got to her feet and went to open. "Toby. Are you here to heal my son?" she asked.

"I'm sure going to try." There was a pause, then Toby said, "You should get some rest. You look tired."

Basil's mother laughed. "What is it with you boys telling me I look tired? I'm going to get offended."

"I know you worry about Basil. We all do, but it's nothing next to what you have to be feeling. Still, he's in good hands. I can promise you that. Sam and I are doing everything we can, and so is Naila. You should get some rest, now that you have the opportunity."

Basil saw his mother's shoulders slump, and he knew she would obey. Toby wasn't speaking as the alpha mate, but there was still an undercurrent of authority in his voice. Besides, he was right. Basil and his mom weren't alone anymore. They had support, people who could take care of Basil if she couldn't. It wasn't easy, but she could finally relax and get some sleep. Even if Basil ended up dying, he would be peaceful, because he knew his mom wouldn't be alone anymore.

"I could stay until you're done," she suggested.

"Or you could go to sleep right away. I promise that if anything happens, we'll let you know. Sam and I would prefer some privacy to do this, though. It's nothing against you. I would be kicking Lucian out, too, if he were here."

Basil rested against his pillows and smiled. Lucian had spent a lot of time with him since he'd arrived a few days ago. He was here to see his brother, but he was neglecting Owen, which was why Basil had told him to spend some time with him. Lucian had tried to protest, pointing out that Basil was sick and needed him, but Basil had countered that his mom would be there if he needed anything.

He loved both of them, albeit differently. He understood why they were worried, and he was grateful for their presence in his life. Still, sometimes, they could be overbearing.

"Get some sleep, Clymene," Naila's voice rang out in the hallway. "We'll take care of your boy. You can trust us."

"I do." Basil's mom turned to look at him. "I'm going to do what they say and go to bed. You'll be fine?"

This time, Basil's smile was more natural. "I will. Have a good nap, Mom."

She stared at him for a while longer. Then she stepped into the hallway, and Basil allowed himself to close his eyes for a moment.

He didn't have long, though. Naila walked in, followed by Toby and Sam. He could hear them talk and the door close, and he knew that while he would be able to rest once they were done, for now, he had to focus on what was happening.

He opened his eyes and straightened, pressing harder against the pillows behind his back. "Do you have any news?"

Toby and Sam looked at each other. "We don't," Toby said. "It's not going to stop us from trying."

"I know. I'm grateful, but I don't want you to overwork yourself."

Toby arched a brow. "Are you trying to tell me what to do?"

"Of course not, Alpha Mate."

Toby grimaced. "Never mind that." He walked around the bed while Sam came to stand next to Basil. They surrounded him, and Basil knew they would try healing him with their hands like they already had a few times. "You know the drill," Toby continued.

Basil nodded. "Stay still, don't say anything, let you work."

Toby grinned. "Exactly."

Basil closed his eyes again. He found it easier to go through this when he couldn't watch the brothers. There was nothing much to watch anyway. He'd been curious the first time, because he'd never seen anything like that, but now he knew that glowing hands and focus weren't going to help. Even the brothers couldn't do anything for him, and he was resigned.

That didn't mean he was going to stop them from trying.

40

He wasn't sure how long it took, but he jerked when a gentle hand touched his shoulder. He blinked his eyes open, knowing nothing had happened when he saw Toby's expression. "It's fine," he said.

Toby shook his head. "It's not. I don't understand why we aren't able to do this."

"I could try calling that unicorn shifter I contacted to help teach you healing," Naila said.

"You said he was busy," Sam pointed out.

"That's doesn't mean he wouldn't be able to help. I'm sure he'd be curious about Basil's case."

"We'll try calling him if nothing else works," Toby finally said. "You should contact him again anyway, to make sure he's actually going to come. It's taking a while."

"Not everyone is at your beck and call, Alpha Mate," Naila teased.

"Will you stop calling me that? Even Basil is, and I hate it."

Basil pressed his lips together. He knew Toby felt awkward in the role, but he was doing a good job. Right now, he was focusing on Basil, and it wasn't like Basil had seen much outside the bedroom he'd been in since he'd arrived, but he liked Toby. He was young, but he would grow into the role, and he would be perfect.

Sam patted Basil's hand. "We'll find a way," he promised.

Basil hoped he was right. He'd just found his mate, and maybe even a family. He didn't want to lose all of that before he could enjoy it.

Lucian was nervous. He should probably have told Basil what he was doing before doing it, but it was too late now.

He looked at his family. As soon as he'd realized how sick Basil was, he'd called his mom. He hadn't expected her to pack up their entire family and come to Rosewood, but that was what she'd done, and now she, along with Lucian's father, his grandparents, and his sister, were standing in the Rosewood pack alpha's living room. The kids were there, too, but they were playing around pack territory with other children. They were having a blast, and it gave the adults time to deal with this. Lucian's brother-in-law had stayed behind to take care of their small pack, but he was just as eager to meet Basil as the rest of them.

"I can't wait to meet him," Lucian's mom said. "And his mother, of course. I can't believe what everyone did to that poor woman."

Lucian grimaced. "I should probably tell them about you before you go barging in."

She scowled at him. "Then go ahead and tell them. We'll be waiting here, but not for long."

Lucian made his way to Basil's bedroom as fast as possible. He got there just as the door opened and Naila, Sam, and Toby walked out. Lucian wanted to go inside and see his mate, but since the healers were there and Basil had allowed them to tell everything to Lucian, Lucian stopped to ask them what was going on.

Toby shrugged, but Lucian could see he was hurting. "Nothing. We tried healing him again, but we had the same result as the last time we did it."

Which was none. "Do you have any clue as to what's happening to him?"

"Not any more than before." Toby sighed. "I hate this. I want to help him, but I don't know how."

"At least you managed to convince Clymene to get some rest," Sam pointed out.

It was a relief. Lucian had seen how tired the woman was when he'd met her, and he'd promised her that while she was resting, he would be the one taking care of Basil. He intended to do just that. "I'm going to talk to him," he said.

"Don't tire him too much," Naila warned. "Since we don't know what's going on with him, we need to be careful."

Lucian grimaced. "Maybe it wasn't such a good idea to call my parents after all."

Naila narrowed her eyes. "Do they want to talk to him?"

"They want to meet him. They're here, along with my grandparents and my sister. I already talked to Camden, and he's okay with all of them staying for a few days. They can't stay long anyway, since they have to go back to the pack."

Naila sighed. "I suppose I can't stop this from happening. Make sure he's not too tired, though."

"I promise." Basil's well-being was the most important thing to Lucian, so the promise wasn't empty.

He snuck into the bedroom, closing the door behind himself. Basil's eyes were closed when Lucian stepped in, but he opened them, and when he saw Lucian, he smiled. "I was wondering where you'd disappeared to. I told my mom you'd keep an eye on me while she was napping, and I didn't want to lie to her."

"I'm not going anywhere. I just had to meet someone."

Basil looked interested. "Someone?"

Lucian rubbed the back of his neck. "I told my parents about you. I also told them you were sick and that no one knew what was going on with you, and they decided to come to Rosewood."

Basil's eyes widened. "You mean they're here?"

"They are, along with my grandparents and my sister. You don't have to meet them if you don't want to, and I warned them that your illness makes it hard for you to meet a lot of people, so they'll understand if you can only talk to them for a few minutes. They're worried, though."

"Why? They don't know me."

"They don't, but they know me, and you're my mate. That's why they're worried. They want me to be happy, and they know that I won't be if you die. More importantly, they would be worried about anyone being sick."

"It's hard to believe that." Basil straightened. "But sure. I want to meet them."

Lucian waited for a second to make sure Basil didn't change his mind. When he didn't, he strode back to the door and opened it. He peeked out, and sure enough, his mother and his sister were there. He wasn't even surprised.

He rolled his eyes. "You can grab Dad and Grandpa and Grandma. Basil wants to meet all of you. Remember my warnings, though."

Lucian's mom didn't even wait. She pushed past him, shaking her head. "We're not deaf. We heard you, and we'll be careful."

By the time Lucian stepped back into the bedroom, introductions were finished and Basil's bed was surrounded. He looked a bit lost, but like everyone had promised, they weren't being pushy. Lucian's mom was fussing over Basil, giving him a glass of water and tucking his blankets around him. She was mothering him, and it made Lucian smile.

"Do you know what's going on with him?" Lucian's grandfather asked.

"We don't. I talked to Toby and Sam again just a few minutes ago, but they still haven't been able to do anything."

Lucian's grandfather frowned. "How is it possible that no one knows what kind of illness he has?"

"We have no idea. We only know the symptoms, which isn't useful right now. He's tired and in pain. He has a hard time eating and sleeping, but that's probably linked to the pain." Lucian hesitated. "He told me that when the pain is the strongest, he feels like he's being torn apart on the inside. I don't know what kind of illness does that, but I wish I could do more to help him. As it is, Naila thinks he only has a few weeks left." And that terrified Lucian. He'd just found Basil.

They were supposed to fall in love and have a lifetime together.

His grandfather hummed. "I see. Well, we'll do everything we can, of course. I can't make any promises, but I might have a way to help."

Lucian turned around to face his grandfather. "What are you talking about?"

"Let's go sit next to him. He needs to hear this. Everyone does."

Lucian's heart raced as he and his grandfather stepped closer to the bed. Lucian was surprised when his mother stepped away to leave him the spot right next to Basil, and he took it, gently linking his fingers with Basil's.

"I'm glad you called them," Basil murmured.

"I'm glad I did, too." Because while Lucian wanted to be there for his mate, he also knew he needed someone to be there for *him*.

"Basil, do you know what kind of shifter Lucian is?" Lucian's grandfather asked.

Basil frowned, but he answered. "A dire wolf."

"Exactly. We're a rare kind of shifter, as I'm sure you're aware. It hasn't been easy, which is one of the reasons I belong to a network of rare shifters. It's comprised of dire wolves, but also unicorns, phoenix, any rare shifter you can think of."

"Are gorgons part of it?"

Lucian's grandfather smiled. "A few of them, yes. They're not who I was thinking about, though."

"Who were you thinking about?" Lucian asked.

"Caladrius."

Lucian looked around, but he wasn't the only one who didn't know what his grandfather was talking about.

"What's that?" Lucian's sister asked.

"Caladrius shifters are even rarer than dire wolves and unicorns. I know of a few of them, but only one is part of this network."

"That doesn't explain what they are," Lucian pointed out.

His grandfather glared at him, but there was no heat in it. "I was getting there. They're white bird shifters. It's not only that, though. They're healers. I've never seen it happen, but I know they take the illness into themselves and fly away, dispersing it."

"That's interesting," Basil slowly said as if he didn't quite understand.

"I just thought it might be worth a shot. Not even two unicorn shifters can help you. If we don't do something, you'll get even sicker, and I don't want that to happen. I can try contacting the caladrius shifter in the network and see what he says."

Lucian and Basil looked at each other. Basil nodded. "I suppose it's worth a shot," he agreed. "It's not like I have anything to lose anyway."

Lucian didn't like hearing him talk that way, but he couldn't deny it was the truth. Basil didn't have a lot of time or opportunities. If they wanted to heal him, they needed to try everything, including contacting this shifter.

Basil was afraid to hope. He'd never heard of caladrius shifters, and he didn't know if anything was going to come out of it. He'd hoped the unicorn shifters would be able to heal him, but that hope had been thwarted, so he was back to square one. The same could happen with this new shifter, so he would have to make sure not to obsess over it the way he wanted to.

Arvin—Lucian's grandfather—smiled. "Good. I'll try contacting him as soon as possible. Even if I can't talk to him, I might be able to find his location. Anything could help at this point."

"Thank you."

Arvin gently patted Basil's hand. "Don't worry about it. You're family. We do everything for family."

It was overwhelming. Basil had only ever had his mother, and now he had all these other people. It wasn't just Lucian's family, either. He'd been surprised, because they'd met only five minutes ago, yet they already treated him like he was truly part of them. Lucian's mother and sister had fussed over him, making sure he was comfortable, while Lucian's father had smiled and nodded and asked him how he was. Lucian's grandparents had given him space, something for which he was grateful. He was having a hard time dealing with everyone, but he wouldn't admit it.

He wanted them to continue fussing. He wanted to feel part of their family, to feel like if he died—*when* he died—someone would mourn him. He was also relieved to know that his mother wouldn't be alone even if something happened to him.

Camden had promised she'd be allowed to stay in Rosewood, and that made Basil feel better. He didn't know whether anything would come out of this caladrius shifter, but even if it didn't, his mother would have a home.

They'd never had that, not really. His mom had stayed in hiding, knowing that if anyone found out a gorgon had had a son, people would try getting their hands on Basil. It was already hard enough dealing with the fact that because his mother was such a rare kind of shifter, people were hunting her. They'd had to move a lot, but now they wouldn't have to anymore. They could stay in Rosewood and be happy.

At least for whatever amount of time Basil still had left. He didn't know how long that was, and he would try anything he could to get better, but even if he couldn't, he was at peace.

"Are you okay?" Lucian asked in a whisper. "I know they're a lot, but they love you."

Basil didn't ask how that was possible given they didn't know him. He was starting to understand that some people were just naturally loving. The pack had welcomed him and his mother, and so had Lucian's family. "I'm fine."

"You look tired."

"I am a bit, but the only thing I've done since I arrived is rest, and I could use a change. It's nice to have them around."

"And they're not even all here. I don't know where Owen is, but he offered to keep an eye on the kids. He'll be here soon, though. There's also Sylvia's husband, who stayed back to take care of the pack."

Owen was just as gentle as the rest of his family, and just as friendly. Basil still wasn't sure about Owen's mate, but he could understand where Lennox was coming from. Lennox was wary and quiet, just like Basil. Well, probably more so. Basil supposed it came from the fact that, unlike Lennox, people didn't think he was a homicidal maniac just because he was a phoenix shifter.

Basil squeezed Lucian's hand and tuned back into the conversation going on around him. Everyone had turned to Arvin, and they were interrogating him about this new shifter he'd brought up. Basil was just as curious, and while he had his own questions, he was happy just sitting back and listening.

"How have I never heard about this?" Marissa, Lucian's mom, asked.

"I just told you, it's because of how rare they are," Arvin answered. He sounded exasperated, which made sense, since he didn't seem to have any more information than what he'd already told them.

"But we know about unicorn shifters. We know about gorgons. Why don't we know about those bird shifters?"

"Because they can heal anything. It's not like unicorn shifters, who focus on wounds and broken bones. They can heal cancer, any kind of illness. It's a dangerous gift to have, and it's not surprising that they are careful."

"Yet you know about one." Marissa sounded skeptical.

"I only do because he's part of the network."

"And what's that about? I'm the future alpha. I should know about this."

Arvin huffed, and it made Basil smile. He'd never had this. He'd never even seen it. Everyone around him belonged to a family, and they behaved like one, teasing and poking at each other, but still loving and gentle.

"I would have told you. It's not like I hear from them every day, or even every week. It's just a support network. If one of us needs anything, the others try to help. I suppose that's why the caladrius shifter is part of it. So far, he hasn't asked for anything, but he might eventually, and he'll know he has people he can count on to support him."

"What could he need?" Eleanor, Lucian's grandmother, asked.

Her husband grimaced. "Well, so far, he's managed to avoid being found. I don't know how, and I'm not about to ask. It's his secret to keep, and I'm more than happy for him to do just that. He might be found one day, though, and when that happens, he'll need someone to rely on. When he does, he can reach out to us. We'll find him a safe place to hide, make sure he's fed and has everything he needs."

"I wish my mother and I had been part of the network," Basil said.

The only one who heard him was Lucian, and he leaned closer, gently kissing Basil's forehead. They hadn't done much more since they'd met, even though Basil desperately wanted to. He wanted to experience everything with his mate. He didn't know how much time he had left, and he didn't want to die without knowing what it felt like to be wrapped around Lucian, maybe to have Lucian inside of him, to be one with him. He hadn't asked, though, and Lucian hadn't offered.

Lucian was no doubt terrified of hurting Basil. Basil could understand where he was coming from, but he wished Lucian could forget he was sick for one second and focus on him as a man, not as a sick person. That wouldn't happen unless Basil healed, though, and Basil had made his peace with it. Still, he wanted more than holding hands and a few kisses on the forehead or cheek. When Lucian started straightening up, Basil grabbed his t-shirt and pulled him back down, pressing their lips together.

Lucian's eyes widened before slowly closing, and then he cupped the back of Basil's head, holding him close as they kissed. It was nothing like what Basil wanted, yet it was also everything. It was gentle and sweet, and even though he wanted to deepen the kiss, he knew better than to do that when Lucian's family was in the room with them.

When they stopped kissing, Lucian stayed close, pressing their foreheads together. "I didn't expect that," he murmured.

"It was an impulse," Basil admitted.

Lucian chuckled. "Well, feel free to do that anytime you want."

"I can?"

"Of course. I'm sorry if this was what you wanted the entire time and I haven't been giving it to you. I'm just not sure how to behave."

And there was Basil's illness again. "I know that asking you to behave as if I'm not sick isn't going to help, but can you forget about it when we're alone? I want more kisses. I want snuggling." He wanted everything he would lose when he died.

Lucian smiled. "All right. I can do that."

"Thank you."

"You don't have anything to thank me for." Lucian kissed

Basil again. "I would give you the world if I could. I would give you anything."

Basil knew it was the truth. He and Lucian might have just met, but Basil had been spending most of his time resting in bed, and Lucian had been next to him the entire time. They'd had the opportunity to talk about everything and anything, and they'd taken it.

Basil was still afraid that Lucian was going to be hurt when he died, but he couldn't stop. It was selfish, but he was dying. Surely, he could have at least this.

Lucian should have realized Basil needed more than what he'd been giving him. He hadn't, but that didn't matter anymore. Basil wasn't afraid to ask for what he wanted, and that was something Lucian admired.

A knock on the door made all of them turn toward it. It opened, and Basil's mom peeked in. Her eyes widened when she saw how many people were in the room, and she frowned. "Who are you?" she asked.

Basil sucked in a breath. "Mom! Don't be rude."

She stepped in, her hands on her hips. "I'm not rude. I'm worried. You know what Naila and the others said. You need to rest. Why are you having a party in your room?"

Lucian chuckled. He understood why it might look like Basil was having a party, but he really wasn't. "Clymene, this is my family. These are my parents, Marissa and Dan. That's my grandfather, Arvin, and my grandmother, Eleanor. The last one is my sister, Sylvia."

Basil's mother still looked wary, but she nodded. "It's a pleasure to meet all of you. I apologize for being rude."

Lucian's mother shook her head. She rushed to Clymene's side, taking her hands in hers. "Don't worry about it. You're trying to protect your son, and I understand. You're not alone anymore, though. Share the burden with us. We'll protect Basil, too."

From Clymene's expression, Lucian was pretty sure his mom was feeling overwhelmed. He wanted to step in, but Basil wouldn't let go of his hand, so he wasn't going anywhere. Still, he could try to rein his mother in. "Mom, let her breathe."

His mom glared at him. "I'm not doing anything. I'm just making sure Clymene and Basil know they're not alone anymore." She tsked. "You should never have been in the first place."

Clymene blinked. "Do you know what kind of shifter I am?"

Lucian's mom beamed. "I do. I find gorgons fascinating, and I don't understand why your peers shunned you. It wasn't fair, and if I ever meet any of them, I'll make sure they know what I think about them."

Clymene chuckled. She sounded in shock, which was normal when first meeting Lucian's mom. He was pretty sure everyone felt that way.

"Thank you," Clymene said. "You don't have to fight that battle for me, though. I made my peace with it a long time ago. The only important thing right now is Basil and making sure he's okay."

Lucian's mom nodded eagerly. "Of course. My father might have a solution."

Lucian groaned. He understood why his mom wanted Clymene to know, but he was afraid she was giving her too much hope.

No one in the room knew anything about caladrius shifters. Lucian hadn't known they existed, and he was skeptical. He wanted them to be real and for his grandfather to know one of them, but was that the truth? His grandfather would never lie, but someone might lie to him. A shifter who could heal any illness, taking it inside themselves before dispersing it and being fine at the end of it sounded too good to be true.

"I'm glad I met you," Basil murmured.

Lucian turned his attention back to him. He wouldn't be able to get a word in the conversation between his mom and Clymene, especially since everyone else was pitching in. It gave Lucian time to focus on his mate. "I'm glad I met you, too."

"It's more than for me, though. If something happens to me, my mom won't be alone anymore."

Lucian's chest felt painfully tight, but he still forced himself to smile. "Nothing will happen to you."

"We both know that might not be true, but sure, we can act as if I'm perfectly fine for a bit."

"That's not what I meant. I just don't want you to lose hope."

"I'm not. I'll believe I can be healed until my last breath. I *want* to believe it, because it means I can be with you if I do. I still have to think about what will happen if your grandfather can't find that shifter, though."

"I don't want to think about that."

"I don't, either. And maybe I don't have to anymore, since I know my mom won't be alone. I can focus on being with you now."

"I'll give you everything I can," Lucian promised. It wasn't an empty promise. He hadn't lied when he'd told Basil that he wished he could give him the world. He wanted to, and if he couldn't, he wanted to give Basil a way to heal. Maybe his grandfather would manage what Lucian hadn't.

"I think it's time to leave," Sylvia said.

Lucian frowned at her. "What's going on?"

She tilted her chin at Basil. "He's tired. The two of you should spend some time together. We can have this conversation outside, which is probably better, since I'm sure the healers will want to hear it."

Lucian was so grateful he could have kissed his sister. "Thank you."

"Don't get all mopey on me. I'm doing this for Basil, not for you."

Lucian laughed. He knew his sister loved him, but they were still siblings, and they squabbled a lot. "Well, whatever reason you have, thank you."

It took a bit to gather everyone and get them out the door. Luckily for Lucian, Owen was in the hallway and headed toward them when they emerged, and everyone's attention turned to him. Lucian's mom was more than happy to introduce Clymene to her other son, even though Clymene already knew him. Owen looked overwhelmed, and Lucian snickered as he closed the bedroom door behind his family, finally giving him and Basil a little time alone.

He turned and leaned against the door, eyeing his mate. "I can go if you're too tired," he offered.

"I don't want you to."

"Even though you're tired?"

"Even though I'm tired," Basil confirmed. "Actually, since we were talking about cuddling earlier, maybe we could do that?"

Lucian locked the door and moved toward the bed. "I'll do anything you want me to do."

Basil smiled. "I'd be careful with that kind of promise. You might find yourself married to me before you can say no."

Lucian's heart skipped a beat. "I wouldn't say no," he murmured.

Basil had been about to lift the comforter so Lucian could slide under it, but he froze. "What?" he croaked.

Lucian shook his head. He toed off his shoes, then he lifted the comforter himself and slid under it, cuddling close to Basil. It was odd, but a good kind of odd. It was the first time they'd done this, yet they seemed to fit together perfectly, as if they'd been doing it for decades.

Basil buried his face against Lucian's throat just like he had the day they'd met. "You can't say something like that and not explain," he complained.

Lucian chuckled and kissed the top of his head. "There's not much to explain. If you were to propose, I would say yes."

"It doesn't make sense."

"Has love ever made sense?"

Basil tilted his head so he could look at Lucian. "We haven't been together long enough to be in love."

"Who says that? A few minutes are enough to fall in love." And Lucian knew he'd been in love with Basil since he'd carried him to his car that night in the rain. It was too soon to tell Basil, though. He was fragile, and even though Lucian didn't know him well, he knew Basil would freak out if he said those three little words.

Basil stared at Lucian for a moment. "I suppose you're right. I can't deny I feel something for you, even though I barely know you."

"See? I was right."

"You were. I still don't think we should get married, though. It wouldn't be fair to you."

Basil hadn't expected them to actually get married, but he wasn't surprised. He was a bit sad, though. "You can't decide what's fair to me or isn't," he pointed out. "But fine. We don't have to get married if you don't want to."

"I never said I didn't want to," Basil murmured as he settled against Lucian's chest again.

Lucian tightened his arms around him. He didn't know what this conversation meant, and maybe it didn't mean anything. Still, he wanted Basil to know how he felt about him. He understood why Basil felt it wouldn't be fair to Lucian to be with him, but Lucian didn't care about any of that.

He didn't know how long he had with his mate, but he didn't want to be left alone with the regret that they could have had more but hadn't taken that chance.

CHAPTER FOUR

Basil should have stayed away from Lucian. Even though Lucian hadn't said anything, Basil could tell he was falling in love with him. He wished it wasn't happening. He was falling in love with Lucian, too, but he was also feeling sicker and sicker with every day that passed. These days, he was lucky if he managed to get out of bed to go to the bathroom. It wouldn't last forever, though, and once he died, Lucian would be left alone without a mate and the man he was in love with.

Basil had been selfish. He knew no one would berate him for it, least of all Lucian, but he couldn't help but feel guilty. He was a condemned man. There was no way out of this, not anymore. Lucian's grandfather hadn't managed to find the caladrius shifter he'd talked about, and Basil had lost hope. He shouldn't have been hoping in the first place. He should have known better.

He hadn't been able to stop himself.

He also hadn't been able to stop himself when it came to Lucian, and now, Lucian was going to be hurt. It wasn't fair, and if Basil were strong enough, he would start pushing Lucian away. He wasn't, though. He was selfish, and he didn't want to spend the last days of his life on his own.

A light knock on the door made him roll his head on the pillow to look at it. "Yes?"

The door opened, and Lucian peeked in. "I brought you lunch."

Basil groaned. "I'm not hungry."

"You know what Naila said. If you want a painkiller, you're going to have to eat. She doesn't want you to take those on an empty stomach."

"Maybe I shouldn't take them, then."

Lucian frowned and stepped inside. He was carrying a tray, and he put it on the dresser before moving toward Basil. "What are you talking about? You're in pain. Why shouldn't you take painkillers?"

Basil shrugged, and even that hurt. Every movement felt like his chest was being torn apart, and he had to remember not to move. "It's taking the pain away, but that's all it's doing. I'm getting worse every day, Lucian. You have to see that."

Lucian grimaced and sat on the mattress next to Basil. "I know."

"But you don't want to talk about it."

"We can if you want, but I don't think there's a reason for us to."

Basil snorted. "Of course there's a reason. When I die, you'll be left alone. You should start putting some distance between us." Because Basil wouldn't be able to do it. Although, he had to have faith that Lucian could.

Lucian looked horrified. "I'm not going to push you away. You're my mate, and you're sick. What kind of man would I be if I didn't want anything to do with you?"

"A man who protects his heart."

Lucian's expression softened. "I won't lie. It's terrifying, and I can't even think about losing you without freaking out. I'm not going anywhere, though. You're it for me, no matter how long we have."

"It's not fair."

Lucian took Basil's hand and squeezed. "I agree, but there's nothing we can do about it except what we've already been doing. You don't have to take the painkillers if you don't want to, but you should eat anyway. You need your strength."

Basil sighed. "I'll take the painkillers." He wasn't a martyr. He was in pain, and he didn't want to be. He didn't have long, and he wanted to spend the little time he still had with Lucian. He wouldn't be able to enjoy it if he was in pain.

Lucian kissed Basil's forehead and got to his feet to grab the tray. Basil didn't want to eat in bed, though, so he struggled to push the comforter away and get to his feet. The floor was cold under his feet, but it felt good after the warmth of the bed. It made Basil feel more alive.

"What are you doing?" Lucian asked. He put the tray on the nightstand and reached for Basil as if to push him back into bed.

Basil shook his head. "I don't want to spend the rest of my life in bed."

"You need to rest."

"I can rest after lunch. Are the others eating in the kitchen?"

"They are. They understand you can't go, though."

"I *can* go." Basil wasn't too sure about that, but he was going to try anyway.

He had no idea how much longer he had, but he suspected it was days rather than weeks. He didn't want to spend that time hidden away in this bedroom, even though people were coming around to visit him. Lucian and his mother were always with him, of course, but they weren't the only ones. Basil had noticed what this mess was doing to Sam and Toby. They were beating themselves up for not being able to help, and Basil didn't know what to tell them to make them feel better. He doubted anything would at this point.

They tried to heal him every day, and every day, they failed. Basil had accepted that, but they hadn't yet, especially Toby. He seemed to take Basil's illness as a personal offense, and every day, he came up with something new — a new herb, a new painkiller — that might help.

Nothing ever did.

Basil looked up at Lucian. "Please. I need to do this."

Lucian glared at him for a moment, and Basil waited. Lucian wasn't the boss of him, but Basil would need his help if he wanted to get to the kitchen. He wasn't stupid. He was weak, although that had as much to do with the fact that he'd been stuck in bed for weeks as with the illness. Weakness had been the first sign something was wrong with him when he'd gotten sick, so he'd spent a lot of time resting back home and at the motel. He didn't know what he would do if he had to stay one more second in this bedroom, though. Probably scream in frustration.

Lucian's shoulders slumped, and Basil knew he'd won. "Nothing I can say will keep you in that bed, right?" he asked.

Basil shook his head. "It won't. I'll ask Naila to give me whatever pills she has for energy. I didn't take them until now because I didn't want to need them, but I'm getting weaker, and I am *not* going to spend the rest of my short life in this bedroom. We don't have a lot of time, but I want to experience what the world has to offer now that I have you and friends."

"I wish you didn't talk about your death so much," Lucian murmured.

"I just want to accept the inevitable. I don't want to talk about it, either, but it's coming, and I can't outrun it. I'm sorry if it hurts you, and trust me, it hurts me, too, but ignoring it isn't going to help." Basil had to start thinking that he wouldn't be healed and plan accordingly.

So far, the only medicines he'd taken from Naila had been the painkillers. She'd offered other things that would give him more energy, but he hadn't needed them. He was in bed, and no one wanted to see him walking around, not when he was this sick. He'd humored them, knowing they were doing everything they could to help him.

They couldn't do anything, though.

Basil wouldn't be able to do much, but he wanted to sit on the porch and breathe air that smelled of rain. He wanted to sit in the kitchen and have meals with his friends, cuddle a little on the couch with Lucian. For the next few days, he wanted as normal a life as he could get. For that happen, he would need Naila's pills. He was done acting like he was strong, because he wasn't. He was weak, both physically and mentally. He was reaching his breaking point, and he needed to do something about it. He couldn't leave a mess when he died.

"You're going to have to help me," he told Lucian. He reached out, and Lucian didn't even hesitate to take his hand.

"I'll always be there to help you," Lucian said. "You don't even have to ask."

"I know." And Basil did. He wished things were different. He wished he and Lucian could actually get married like they'd talked about the day Basil had met Lucian's family. He wished they had long years in front of them, years in which they could be happy and get to know each other.

Instead, they had mere days, and he would have to make the best out of it.

Lucian almost had to carry Basil to the kitchen. He didn't mind, but he was worried.

He tightened his hold on Basil's waist and pulled him closer as they stumbled forward.

He understood why Basil wanted to do this. He would probably have gone crazy, too, if he'd been stuck in the same room for days. Still, sometimes, he wished Basil wasn't so stubborn.

Of course, if Basil hadn't been stubborn, he probably

wouldn't be here. Naila said she was stunned at how well he was handling this. She was surprised that with everything happening to him, he wasn't sleeping away the time he had left. Instead, he was insisting on going to lunch with the others. Lucian was both proud and terrified, and it was a strange mix of feelings.

He could hear voices coming from the kitchen before they got there. Basil straightened a bit, his feet shuffling forward. He was clearly eager to get there, and Lucian realized that everyone had been keeping him isolated. It wasn't on purpose or because they were mean. They wanted to help him and keep him safe, and they thought they were doing that by keeping him in bed. Maybe they were, but it wasn't what Basil wanted. He was done staying away from life, especially since he didn't have that much of it left.

The thought made Lucian's chest feel tight, and he had to push it away so he wouldn't break down in front of everyone, including Basil.

They walked into the kitchen, and the voices stopped. Everyone stared at them, and Lucian tried to smile. He was pretty sure it came out as a grimace, but it didn't matter. "Basil decided he wanted to join us for lunch," he explained.

Toby, who was the closest to them, shot to his feet. "Why don't you sit here?" he told Basil.

Basil chuckled. "I know I'm weak, but I'm pretty sure I can get to that chair over there," he said, tilting his chin toward an empty chair on the other side of the table.

"I'm sure you can, but why should you have to?"

Basil shook his head. "Sit down, Toby. I can do this. It's probably going to take me the entire lunch to get my energy back after the walk, but I'll be fine."

They started moving again. Basil's body was heavy, but Lucian would have carried him for the rest of his life if that was what he wanted. Once they got to the empty chair, Basil was breathing hard, and he slumped into it. There were beads of sweat on his forehead, but he didn't seem to care as he caught his breath.

Lucian sat in the chair next to him, rubbing his back. He didn't want to make a big affair out of it, because he knew Basil would hate it, but everyone was worried.

"I'll get you a plate," Sam murmured. He got to his feet and headed toward the stove.

Basil didn't try to stop him. Maybe he was accepting that he needed help, after all.

"You did good," Lucian murmured.

Basil grinned at him. "Didn't I? I managed to walk all the way to the kitchen. I had some help, but still. I'm proud of myself."

He wasn't being sarcastic. He truly was happy to be there, and Lucian had to swallow the sob that tried to make its way out of his throat.

Basil was trying to be strong for all of them. He knew how bad they felt about not being able to help him, and he no doubt felt even worse. Still, he was trying to show them that he was as fine as possible considering the circumstances, and the least Lucian could do was trying to act as if nothing was wrong.

He managed until someone knocked on the front door. He shot to his feet, more than happy to be able to leave the kitchen table for a bit. "I'll go," he said, even though it wasn't his house. He was only a guest, but Camden already told him he could stay as long as he wanted, and Toby had agreed.

Lucian took a deep breath once he was out of the kitchen. He'd thought he would be strong enough, but now he wasn't sure anymore. To him, it felt like Basil was stronger than him, even though he was the one dying. Lucian didn't know how to deal with this, and he didn't know if he ever would be able to.

Instead of obsessing over that, he went to open the door. He was stunned to see his grandfather standing there, especially when his grandfather looked at him, grimaced, and pulled him into his arms.

"That bad?" Arvin asked.

Lucian allowed himself to lean against him for just a moment. "It's getting worse." He pushed away and forced himself to smile. "He's in the kitchen having lunch with everyone else. I'm sure he'll be happy to see you."

Arvin nodded. "Everyone is there, then?"

"Naila isn't, but we can call her. What's going on?"

"I found the general area where the caladrius shifter is staying."

Lucian's heart raced. "Only the general area?"

"Only that. I'm sure we can work with it, though." Lucian's grandfather stepped inside, headed to the kitchen, and Lucian quickly followed him after closing the door. Arvin made a beeline for Basil once he got there, leaning close to him and murmuring something to him. Basil smiled, but it was tremulous, and Lucian couldn't stay away.

"My grandfather has news," he announced.

Everyone's attention was on them, but only Basil counted.

"I didn't talk to the caladrius shifter, but I managed to find someone who knows where he is," Arvin said. "I don't have an address yet, just an area, and we're going to have to be fast."

"Where?"

"In Des Moines."

Lucian frowned. "Iowa? That's what? A twenty-four-hour drive?"

"Less, if you go fast," Arvin said. "But yes. It's far, but it's the only chance we have."

"It would be forty-eight hours before the caladrius shifter is here, though, and that's not counting the time it's going to take to convince him to come."

"I have to go," Basil said.

"You can't go. You're not feeling well."

"It doesn't matter. Like you said, it would take too long for the caladrius shifter to come here. I can't afford to waste two entire days, maybe even more. At least if I go, it's only going to take half of that time."

"You can't be serious," Clymene said. She started getting to her feet.

Her son shook his head at her. "Don't you see? I have to do it. I *want* to do it."

Clymene stared at Basil. Lucian could already tell that no one would be able to change Basil's mind, and while he was terrified, he agreed this was the right thing to do. Basil was right — if he wanted a chance to make it, he had to go and see the caladrius shifter himself. It would be much faster, and maybe the caladrius shifter would be more inclined to help Basil if he knew him.

"You can't go alone," Clymene said.

"He won't," Lucian intervened. "I'm going with him."

"So am I," Owen said. Lucian turned to look at him, and Owen smiled. "And Lennox, of course. We're both coming with you. That way, you'll be safe, and we can take turns driving. We'll only have to stop to eat and go to the bathroom."

"One of us should also go," Toby said.

Basil shook his head. "It's no use. I know you're trying to help, but nothing you do is actually doing anything. You and Sam should stay here. I don't think I'll need you, and it's dangerous for you to be out and about. Someone could find out you're a unicorn shifter."

"It's dangerous for you, too," Toby pointed out.

"At this point, everything is dangerous for me. Does it matter? I'm going to die anyway if I don't do anything."

Lucian wanted to reach out and pull Basil into his arms,

but he kept his hands to himself. Basil was vibrating with hope and energy, and it was a huge change from how he'd been the past few days. Lucian was torn between being happy and being terrified—that something would happen during the trip, that Basil might not get there in time, even to hope.

The caladrius shifter was their last chance. If they couldn't find him or couldn't convince him to help, it would be too late for Basil.

Basil was relieved he wouldn't have to go alone. He'd known Lucian would go with him, of course, but it would have been hard for both of them. Basil didn't want Lucian to be alone if the caladrius shifter refused to help him or if they couldn't find him. He wasn't sure he would be coming back from this trip, not alive. Owen was the best person to go with them, since he was Lucian's brother and they were growing close, and Basil smiled gratefully at him.

Owen smiled back, but he was obviously worried.

"I want to come," Basil's mom said.

"It's even more dangerous for you," Basil pointed out.

"So? I've been on my own since you were born. I kept you safe until now, haven't I? I can continue to do it."

Basil knew she was right, but he didn't want her to be there. He didn't want her to see him die. She would try to be strong and tell him she was okay, but he already knew she wouldn't be. It would be even worse if she was there.

"Basil is right," Camden said. When Basil looked at him, he smiled before turning his attention back to Basil's mom. "It would be too dangerous. He's looking for an extremely rare shifter. His presence there will already put the caladrius shifter in more danger than he is now. Having you or Toby or Sam there, too, would make it worse. They only have one chance to talk to this shifter, and I doubt he'll be eager to do it if he's put in even more danger of being found or captured."

"He can't do this alone," Basil's mom said.

Basil wanted to get up and go to her, but he wasn't sure his legs would support him. "I'm not doing this alone, though. I'll have Lucian and Owen and Lennox. I know it's hard to wrap your mind around it, Mom, but we're not alone anymore. We have people who care about us and who are doing everything they can to make sure I'm fine. They'll keep me safe. I'm sure of that."

"Nothing will happen to your son if I have anything to say about it," Lucian said. He sounded fierce.

It was hard not to cry. Lucian would be in so much pain if something happened to Basil, and Basil didn't know how to deal with it. He wasn't sure he could. He already had a hard time dealing with the fact that he was about to die and that it would happen soon. It was terrifying, sad, and horrible. Basil wanted to take care of Lucian and make him feel better, but he didn't know if he could do it for himself, let alone for someone else.

Camden cleared his throat. "I think the four of them should go alone. Lennox, call your brother and tell him what's happening. He'll want to know. Owen, you need to start packing. I want the four of you to leave this afternoon. The sooner you get there, the better it will be." Camden turned to Lucian and Basil. "As for you, you need to call Naila. She has to know what's happening, too. She'll want to give you medicines. I know you haven't been taking all of them, but now isn't the time to say no. You'll need all your energy and not to be in pain for this."

Basil nodded. "I know. I'll take anything she wants me to take."

Camden smiled. "Good. Lucian, I know I don't have to tell you this, but you should help him get ready." He paused and frowned. "Although of course, you don't have to obey.

Neither of you is a pack member."

"We'll obey," Lucian said.

Basil agreed. He wanted to be a pack member, but he knew better than to ask right now. He might not come back from this trip. If that was the case, Lucian would go back to his family, so it would be pointless to ask to stay in Rosewood now.

Owen and Lennox got to their feet, leaving the kitchen quickly. Basil had to go more slowly, but Lucian was there once again. He wasn't the only one, either. His grandfather was talking with Camden and Toby, but Basil's mom rushed to his side. Together, she and Lucian helped him get back to the bedroom, and Basil had never been so happy to see that bed.

His mom was about to cry, and he wished there was something he could say or do to reassure her. They both knew what he'd have to face, though. Basil was in pain, both physically and mentally, and he was weak, but he had to do this. He would have to convince his mother to stay.

"I don't want to let you go," she murmured once Lucian turned his attention to the dresser to start packing.

"I have to."

"But there's no reason for me not to go with you. We both know . . ."

That he might not come back. Basil swallowed heavily. "That's why I don't want you to come. I know it might sound cruel, but I don't want you to remember me that way. You've been taking care of me for so long, and I know we don't have a lot of good memories since this illness started, but I want you to remember the good times, not the bad ones."

A tear rolled down her cheek, and Basil reached out to catch it with his index finger. "I know you're an adult now," she said, choking on the words. "I can't force you to allow me to go with you, no matter how much I want to. Just remember that I will always love you, whatever happens."

"I already knew that, Mom. You don't have to tell me. I'll always love you, too."

A sob escaped her, and she threw herself into Basil's arms. He wrapped them around her, holding her close as they both wept.

He didn't know if he would ever see her again, and he didn't know how to deal with it. She'd always been there for him. Before they met Lucian and the others, they'd been everything to each other. They'd never needed anyone else, or at least, that was what Basil had thought. Now, he realized he'd been wrong.

Even if he died, he wouldn't die unhappy. In his quest to find a cure, he'd found a family for both himself and his mother, and it would be worth it. She wouldn't be alone ever again, and Basil couldn't regret getting sick, not when this was the result.

"Come back to me," his mom murmured. "You hear that?" She straightened and looked him in the eyes. "You have to come back to me."

"I'll do everything I can."

"Promise me, Basil. Promise me you'll come back."

Basil wanted to give her what she wanted, but he knew better. He didn't want to make a promise he wouldn't be able to keep. Instead, he kissed her cheek and hugged her again, sending the scent of her perfume to memory. "I love you."

She stared at him for a moment. Then, she nodded and looked at Lucian. "You keep my baby safe. Understood?"

Lucian had been pushing clothes into Basil's backpack, but he turned to look at her. "I'll do everything I can to bring him back and keep him safe. I promise."

"I know you will. He's as important to you as he is to me."

Basil's heart felt like it was about to explode with love and sorrow. He didn't want to lose this. He wanted to stay here, to bask in the love of these people. Instead, he was probably going to die miles away from here.

At least he wouldn't be alone. Lucian had promised to stay with Basil until the end, and Basil believed him. Either way, they were doing this together.

Lucian was terrified. Whatever happened on this trip was going to change his life forever. Either he would lose Basil, or they would both come back and spend the rest of his life together.

If that was what happened, he was marrying his mate.

By the time they were ready, Basil looked better. Naila had spent time with him, stuffing him full of medicines and packing as many of them as possible for them to take. It was going to be a long car trip, but they hadn't been able to find flights that would get them to their destination faster. This was all they could do, and Lucian already knew that when he'd drive, he wouldn't respect the speed limit.

Which was probably why Owen had told him he wasn't touching the steering wheel.

"I wish I could do more," Lucian's grandfather said. He sounded sad, and Lucian wanted to tell him he didn't have to feel guilty.

"You did a lot. If we manage to do this, it will be thanks to you."

"I don't like seeing him this way. I want him to be okay and for you to be happy." He hesitated. "If anything happens, will you come home?"

Lucian couldn't imagine going anywhere else. He loved being in Rosewood, and he was pretty sure that if Basil made it, both of them would move here, but if he didn't, he didn't know if he would be able to come back. "I will."

"Your mom wanted to be here, but we didn't want to overwhelm you and Basil. They're all thinking of you, though.

Both of you."

"I know. I'm grateful." Both that his family was thinking about them and that they weren't there. Lucian was trying hard not to break down. He needed to be strong for Basil, but it was the hardest thing he'd ever done.

His grandfather pulled him into a strong hug. "I wish I could promise you everything will be okay, but I have no way to know. What I do know is that you're not alone. Whatever happens, you'll have support and love."

Lucian needed to get out of this place. If he didn't, he was going to break down crying, and that was the last thing he needed. Basil wasn't crying, and Lucian shouldn't be, either.

He swallowed. "I'll do everything I can to bring him back."

"I know."

"Let us know, whatever happens," Camden said. "If you need anything, we'll be there. Once this is over, don't feel the need to rush back. Take your time, stop at motels, take a breather. You're going to need it after everything that happens." He looked at Basil as he said that.

Lucian wondered if Camden really believed Basil was coming back.

Everyone was trying to be supportive and upbeat, but none of them were doing a good job of it.

"We could take a week coming back once Basil is healed," Owen said. "Maybe have a family vacation?"

"Whatever you need, just let me know," Camden repeated.

"We'll be back soon," Basil said.

He looked better. He was standing on his own, stronger than he had been recently, but he was still pale, and his frown told Lucian that even with the painkillers, he was still in pain. He would probably sleep a lot in the car, but Lucian had nothing against that. If anything, he *wanted* Basil to sleep. Whatever they were going to find when they got to the caladrius shifter, Basil would need all the energy he could muster to face it.

From the look of everyone in the entrance, they knew that Basil might not come back. Still, none of them pointed that out, and Lucian was thankful. Basil's mom was sobbing, with Sam trying to comfort her but not having much success. Lucian doubted any of the people in the room right now would feel better until Basil came back. If he didn't, well, they would face that when—if—it happened.

The way Basil had dug his way into these people's lives, including Lucian's, was incredible. He was such a good person, and everyone loved him. They were going to be destroyed if he didn't come back, which was one of the reasons Lucian knew he would have to stay away. He would need time to mourn his mate and the life they could have had, and being with Basil's mother would make it worse.

Now wasn't the time to think about that. It was time to focus on what they could do to save Basil, and Lucian was relieved when they finally moved toward the front door.

They were taking Lennox's car. It was already packed, both with a backpack for each of them and with food and drinks. They would have to stop eventually, if anything to use the restroom, but they would drive as much as they could before then.

"Keep my baby safe," Clymene murmured when she hugged Lucian.

"I'll do my best," he promised.

She leaned back and smiled. "I know you will."

Lucian had to step away, and he did so, rushing toward the car and opening the back door. Basil and his mother hugged one last time, but it seemed like Basil felt the same way Lucian did. They needed to go, and they needed to go now.

Lucian helped Basil climb into the car, and once he was settled, he closed the door and walked around it to the other back door. Lennox and Owen were still there, and the three of them looked at each other.

"We can do this," Owen said.

"I hope so." Lucian wasn't sure they could, but they would certainly try.

"We'll do our best," Lennox murmured. It was a surprise to hear him speak, and it made Lucian realize that he cared just as much as Owen did. He might not say it out loud, but they were still family, and Lucian had to fight the urge to hug him.

He was pretty sure Lennox wouldn't be happy if he did.

They climbed into the car, and Lucian made sure Basil had everything he needed. Basil rolled his eyes, but he was also smiling, so he probably didn't mind.

"Everyone ready?" Lennox asked from the driver seat.

Basil smiled at him, and the smile was more natural than it had been in the past few days. "As ready as I can be."

Lennox chuckled. "I suppose that's the best any of us can do." He turned the engine on, and Lucian twisted to look at the people waving them off.

Basil's mother was there, with Sam and Toby surrounding her. She was crying, but she was standing tall, and she nodded at Lucian when she saw him watching her. Camden and Lucian's grandfather were next to each other, looking severe. Everyone was worried about Basil, and they all wanted him to come back.

Lucian hadn't let himself hope too much, but now that they were on their way, he did. They had a way to heal Basil. It wasn't going to be easy, but they could do this.

They had to.

Chapter Five

Basil felt like shit after the long car ride. There were positive aspects to that, though. Their little group had arrived in Des Moines, which meant they could start looking for the caladrius shifter.

If only they knew where to start.

They had a general area, but it was still so big. Basil had never lived in a city—too many people who might find out what he and his mother were—and it was overwhelming. The pain and exhaustion made it even worse.

"I wish Arvin had been more precise," Owen said. He stood there, his hands on his hips, looking around.

Basil was pretty sure that wasn't going to help them find the caladrius shifter.

"He did what he could," Lucian said. "We have a neighborhood. The caladrius shifter is hiding somewhere around here, and we have to find him."

"We're certainly going to try, but there's a lot of people and a lot of buildings."

"That's not going to stop me. What about you?"

Owen looked hurt and offended. "Do you really think I would let something like this stop me from finding the only person who can heal your mate?"

Basil didn't want the brothers to fight. If he didn't make it back home, Lucian had to be able to rely on Owen. "I know that everyone here wants to find the caladrius shifter," he said. "We shouldn't fight. It's hard, but we have to focus on finding this shifter."

Owen looked bashful. "You're right. I'm sorry." He peeked at Lucian. "Sometimes, it's still hard to come to terms with the fact that I have a brother and a sister. This isn't how Lucian's vacation in Rosewood was supposed to go."

Basil smiled. "This isn't how a lot of things were supposed to go." He looked around. "All right. Where do we start?"

"We call the closest alpha," Lennox said. Hearing him speak was strange, but it got everyone's attention. He didn't enjoy it, but it wasn't going to stop him. "Camden looked it up, and he gave me the number. We don't know if she's going to be able to help, but it's better than nothing."

They all waited with bated breath as he dialed a number. He looked uncomfortable, but since he was officially Camden's envoy, he was the one who would have to talk to the alpha.

"Alpha Johnson. My name is Lennox, and I'm a member of the Rosewood pack."

Basil moved even closer in the hope that he'd hear what she was saying. It would have been good to put her on speaker, but they weren't in the car anymore, and they couldn't afford for anyone to overhear the conversation.

"You're far from home," she said. Her voice was barely more than a whisper for Basil, but it was enough.

"My friends and I are looking for something, or rather, someone."

"Which is why you called. What can I do for you?"

"Do you know anything about a caladrius shifter?"

There was a pause before she answered. "It's been a long time since I heard that name. Are you sick?"

"Not me, but someone close to me. A family member. Nothing else we did helped, and we don't have a lot of time."

"I don't know if there's a caladrius shifter in my area, even outside the pack. I do know of a few shifters that tend to gather in the same buildings. When they're not part of any pack or shifter group, it's safer for them. I can tell you which buildings those are, but I don't think there's anything else I can do for you."

Basil looked around. He supposed that knocking on every door in two or three buildings would be easier than doing so for hundreds. This was the only clue they had as to where the caladrius shifter might be. Of course, that was if he actually stayed around with shifters. He might not, considering what kind of shifter he was. If he was lucky, he'd found other rare shifters and lived with them or close to them. If he wasn't, he would have to hide from other shifters, which would make it even harder to find him.

By the time Basil turned his attention back to Lennox, he'd hung up. He didn't put his phone away, though, staring at the screen instead. His lips curled into a tiny smile, and he turned the screen so Basil and the others could see it. "She sent me the address of the buildings she was talking about. There are only three of them, and even if there are hundreds of doors there, we might be able to find the shifter." He hesitated. "We should probably separate. It would make it faster to knock on all those doors and talk to people."

"You're here to protect Basil," Owen pointed out.

"I am, and I can stay with them, but this would be faster."

"I can go on my own while you go with Basil and Lucian."

Lennox's expression told Basil what he thought of that suggestion. "I'm not letting you knock on doors alone. We don't know who lives in those apartments."

Owen crossed his arms over his chest. "Then we'll go together. I know we have to be quick, but it's not going to help if one of us is attacked. We don't know how the caladrius shifter will react to our presence here, or any other shifter who might open their door. If they avoid being in a pack, they probably have a good reason for that. They could be dangerous, and they might not take it kindly to a shifter knocking on their door and asking who they are and if they know this caladrius shifter." He looked at Basil, and his expression shifted to worry. "I'm sorry."

Basil shook his head. "I understand, and to be honest, I don't think we should separate, either. Sticking together will be the safest." He hoped it wouldn't lead to his death, but if it did, he had made his peace with it.

It was strange. Basil had thought he'd made his peace with death when he'd realized that nothing he and his mother came up with helped. Then he'd met Lucian and the others, and he hadn't been as okay with dying as he'd been before. He stood to lose a lot more now, but he also couldn't deny that his death was probably inevitable. This was the last chance for Basil to make it out alive, and he knew that Owen, Lucian, and Lennox would do everything they could to find this shifter. If they couldn't, Basil would die.

He didn't want to. It was hard to get used to that idea, but he supposed he was lucky he'd had at least some time with his mate. He knew what love was now. He wished Lucian wouldn't be left alone once he was gone, but even when Basil died, he would have his brother, the rest of his family, and the Rosewood pack if he managed to go back to them. Even Basil's mother wouldn't be alone anymore.

Basil could die in peace, even though he didn't want to.

"We should start," Lennox said.

Basil swallowed and nodded. "Where to? You're the leader here."

Lennox didn't look happy about that, but he nodded and pointed at a building. "This is the closest one. Hopefully, we'll find the shifter here. If we don't, we can move on to the other two."

He turned toward the building, and Basil moved to follow him. Lucian caught his hand, though, and brought it to his lips to kiss the back of it. "You sure you're feeling okay?" he asked.

"As okay as possible in this situation. What about you?"

"I'm not the sick one. I'll be fine."

Basil suspected that wasn't the truth, but pointing it out wouldn't help.

"Tell me if you need anything," Lucian murmured. "I know we need to focus, but don't hide pain or anything else from us. It won't help in the long run."

"I'll tell you if I am not feeling well. I promise."

Lucian nodded, and together, they followed Lennox and Owen. Basil didn't know if he would ever feel okay again. He didn't now, no matter what he'd told Lucian, and he hoped things would change for the better. The only way to make that happen was to find the caladrius shifter, and right now, it looked like too big of a mission for only four men.

Lucian had lost count of how many doors they'd knocked on. There'd been dozens, and while they'd been lucky with some, they hadn't with others. Most people were curious and per-plexed when Lucian and Owen explained why they were there. Some had been rude and had slammed the door in their faces. Other doors hadn't opened, which made sense, since the people who lived there were probably at work.

But they still had no idea where the caladrius shifter was.

"We still have two buildings to go through," Lennox said as they left the first one. They'd gone through all six floors and found no caladrius shifter and not even a hint as to where he could be.

Basil's stomach grumbled, and Lucian frowned. "You're hungry," he told his mate.

"I'll survive until we can stop for dinner."

"Or we could stop for dinner now. It might not be a bad idea. That way, some of the people who still aren't home from work will be back. We'll have more luck finding them home and asking them questions."

Basil grimaced. "They probably won't be happy to talk to us after an entire day at work."

"That's not going to stop me." Lucian didn't care how many people were rude to him. He was going to find the caladrius shifter if it was the last thing he did.

"Can we stay out here for a bit first? I'd like some fresh air."

"Why don't you sit on the bench over there," Owen said, pointing. "Lennox and I will go to that fast-food place and get something to eat."

Lennox arched a brow. "I thought you said we should stick together."

Owen glared at him. "I meant while knocking on doors. We won't be far, and we'll be able to keep an eye on them. Besides, they'll only be sitting there. It's not like they're going to ask anyone if they know about this shifter."

Lennox raised his hands. "I apologize for asking."

Owen shook his head. "I shouldn't have snapped. I guess everyone is on edge."

"And it's my fault," Basil murmured.

Lucian didn't think Owen and Lennox had heard him, which was why he waited for them to be gone to turn to his mate and ask, "You know it's *not* your fault, right?"

Basil looked a little surprised that Lucian had heard him, or maybe that Lucian thought that. "They wouldn't be fighting if it weren't for me."

"They probably would. They haven't been together long, and they're still finding their way around each other, just like we are. They're mates, but it doesn't mean they're never going to fight."

"We'll fight, too?"

"Of course." If Basil made it out, they no doubt would. Lucian didn't want to think of a world in which they wouldn't.

He gestured at the bench. "Come on. Let's go sit down."

Basil allowed Lucian to drag him toward the bench. Lucian was relieved, yet at the same time, worried. He could see that Basil was getting tired, which meant they would probably have to stop for the night. It wasn't just for Basil—the people living in the apartments they were visiting would eventually go to bed, and Lucian felt a bit panicky at the thought.

They had to find the caladrius shifter, if not today, then tomorrow. Basil was holding up with the medicines Naila had given him, but it wouldn't last forever. Eventually his body would become weaker and the pain too strong. Basil would have to stop, and when he did, Lucian wasn't sure he would be able to get back on his feet.

They sat on the bench. Lucian wrapped his arm around Basil's shoulder and pulled him close. Basil leaned against him, sighing in what had to be a relief to be off his feet.

"You should have told me you were getting so tired," Lucian gently scolded.

"What good would it have done? It's not like we can stop even if I get tired."

Lucian wished he could tell Basil he was wrong, but they both knew he wasn't. Instead of answering, he kissed the top of Basil's head and held him closer. He looked around, wondering how long it would take Owen and Lennox to be back. He and Basil weren't uncomfortable here, although some of the pigeons seemed to think they were about to eat and were gathering around them, no doubt to get a snack. One of them, a white one, even came close enough to catch Lucian's shoelace with his beak. Lucian made sure not to hurt it as he shooed it away, shaking his foot. The pigeon didn't seem to care much, though. It cocked his head and stared at Lucian until Lucian had to look away.

It was better to focus on Basil anyway. Who cared about the pigeons?

"Here you go," Owen said when he and Lennox came back. "We forgot to ask what you guys wanted, so we got a bit of everything. There's salad, burgers, a few wraps, and of course, fries."

Lennox put a hand on Owen's shoulder and squeezed. "Let them breathe," he murmured.

Owen's cheeks went red, and while Lucian knew he was embarrassed, he was grateful for how caring his brother was. Once all of this was over and Basil felt better, Lucian wanted to spend some time with Owen. They'd lost so many years because of the man who had kidnapped him. Now, they were losing the time they were supposed to spend together, and it felt like it was still that man's fault. Neither of them cared because it was for Basil's sake, but still.

Lennox and Owen sat on the bench, too, even though it was a tight fit. They ate, but Basil didn't seem to be hungry, and Lucian was worried. He gently coaxed his mate into eating more, knowing that Basil needed the energy from the food.

"What now?" Owen asked.

"There's not much to do but continue knocking on doors," Lennox answered.

"It's getting late, though. People aren't going to be happy to see us. They already weren't, at least some of them."

"We're going to have to find a hotel somewhere," Lucian intervened. "We can start knocking on more doors, but I doubt we'll be able to go through an entire building tonight. Basil is getting tired. He's going to need sleep and a comfortable place to rest."

Lucian turned his attention back to his mate. Basil was nibbling on his burger, not paying attention to the conversation, and staring at the pigeons instead. He was too pale, and his hands trembled as he moved. He was getting weak, but Lucian didn't know how to help him.

They didn't have a choice. They had to do this to help Basil, no matter how much it hurt him. It was torture for Lucian to have to choose.

"Maybe we could find a hotel now and leave the two of you there," Owen suggested.

"We shouldn't separate," Lucian said automatically.

"You wouldn't be in danger in a hotel room. You can lay low while Lennox and I poke around. Hopefully, we'll find the shifter and bring him back to the hotel."

"What if he wants to meet Basil first?"

"Then we'll call you, and we can come to you, or you can come to us."

"I want to continue," Basil said.

Lucian hadn't realized he was listening in to the conversation, but he should have known better. He also should have known better than hoping Basil would agree to this plan. "You need rest," he pointed out.

Basil glared, but there was no heat in it. "I'll get it eventually. We have to make the most of the time we have, though. I'll be fine."

"I'm not sure you will be," Lucian murmured.

"I'll have to be. I'll take another pill for the pain. It'll make things easier. I can do this."

Lucian sighed. "I know you can. You're the strongest person I've ever met. You can do everything you want." Lucian wasn't sure Basil's body would go along with it, though.

"We can continue for a few more hours," Lennox intervened. "After that, it will be too late, and people won't be opening their doors anymore. We can start again tomorrow morning."

Lucian nodded, then turned his attention back to Basil. He'd only eaten a bit of his burger, and Lucian knew that pushing him to eat more wouldn't work. Instead, when Basil handed it to him, he wrapped it and put it back into the paper bag it had come in. Then he gathered Basil into his arms again.

He took a deep breath, sending Basil's scent to memory.

He didn't know how much longer he would still be able to smell that scent, to feel how Basil fit against him, to listen to the slow beating of his heart. He had to make the most of it now that he could, but knowing that filled him with dread.

Basil needed a moment to rest. He leaned harder against Lucian, knowing that his mate would hold him up and keep him safe. He'd thought that stopping for a moment to eat would help, but instead, the bit of the burger he'd managed to choke down made him feel like he was going to throw up. All the food made him feel that way nowadays, but Basil needed his strength to continue this.

They were no closer to finding the caladrius shifter than they'd been when they'd arrived. They didn't even have a name, which made it even harder. It was hard to explain to the people who opened their doors what and who they were looking for. Most of them were humans, and they had to be vague and ask about a healer. Since the caladrius was so careful, they could probably use scents and skip the humans at once, but they didn't want to, because they might know something. It was a complicated situation, and it wasn't going to get easier.

Basil looked up at the buildings around them. They'd finished one, but there were others. They wouldn't be able to knock on every single door.

As he lowered his gaze, he noticed a man coming toward them. He frowned and looked around, wondering if maybe instead of toward them, the man was walking toward someone else. There were a lot of people around now that it was getting later, and the area in which they were had a few restaurants. They were filling up with people, so it was entirely possible that this man was headed somewhere.

It did look like he was headed straight for the bench where they were sitting, though.

Basil was the only one who had noticed so far, and he didn't say anything. Instead, he kept an eye on the man.

He was small, so Basil doubted he would do anything to hurt them. He could be wrong, but the man looked harmless. His hair was a shocking white-blond, and it fell in front of his eyes. He was wearing jeans and a jacket, both too big for him. He looked a bit like a child wearing his father's clothes, but that didn't make him dangerous.

The fact that he stopped right in front of their bench might, though.

Lennox was on his feet in seconds. He stepped in front of Basil, Lucian, and Owen. His stance told everyone that he wouldn't hesitate to become violent if he needed to protect them.

The man didn't seem to care. He tried to peek around Lennox, his focus on Basil.

Basil straightened. Pain filled his chest, and he grimaced, but he tried to push it away. He really needed to take one of those pills before the pain made it impossible for him to continue.

"What do you want?" Lennox asked.

"To talk to him," the man answered.

"Why do you want to talk to him?" Lennox peeked behind himself. "Basil? You know this guy?"

Basil shook his head. "I've never seen him before."

"What do you have?" The man asked. "Cancer? Something else?"

Basil opened his mouth, but only a croak came out.

"How do you know he's sick?" Lucian asked. He was still holding Basil, but he was tense now.

"It's obvious."

Basil couldn't deny that was probably the truth. He was

shaky, and he had no doubt he was also pale. He probably looked like he was about to faint. This guy had probably happened to walk by and was worried. It didn't make a lot of sense, but Basil couldn't allow himself to hope for something else.

"I don't know what I have," he murmured. He looked at the man, wishing he had an answer for him—and himself. If he did, he would know whether or not he could be healed. "But it's painful. It's making me weak."

The man nodded. "I can see that. I'm sorry."

"Thank you."

The man didn't go away, though. He kept staring at Basil, although his gaze sometimes jumped to the other three in their group. He didn't spend a lot of time on Lennox, which was strange, since Lennox was still standing there and was clearly dangerous.

"What about the other three of you?" the man eventually asked. "You don't look sick."

"We're not," Lucian told him. "We just want to help Basil. We're here to support him."

The man scrunched his nose. "Basil?"

"It's my name," Basil confirmed.

"Why are you named like an herb?"

Lucian tensed even more, but the man's words made Basil smile. "My mom said that she craved basil when she was pregnant with me. When she found out she was having a boy, it felt natural to call me that."

"I'm not sure whether that's a cute story or a horrifying one," the man said.

"What do you want?" Lennox asked. "As you know, Basil is sick, and he needs rest. We need to find a hotel."

The man peered at Lennox. He had to crank his neck to be able to look him in the eyes, something that made Basil smile even wider. He didn't know what it was with this man, but

Basil liked him.

"What you need is a healer," he said.

Basil didn't miss how he used the word healer rather than doctor the way humans would. "We've been looking for one," he confirmed.

"Didn't have a lot of luck with that, did you?"

"Not yet, no. And I don't have a lot of time left."

"Was there anything you wanted?" Owen asked. From his tone, he was reaching the end of his patience.

Basil felt like they couldn't afford to antagonize this man, though. He cleared his throat, getting everyone's attention. "Like you know, my name is Basil. The man hugging me is my boyfriend, Lucian. The one standing in front of you is Lennox, and the last one is Owen, Lucian's brother. And you are?"

The man looked from one to the other. He stayed silent for a while longer until he seemed to make a decision. "My name is Peregrine."

Basil snorted. "You made fun of me because I'm named for a plant, while you're named for an animal?"

Peregrine grinned. "I wasn't making fun. I was just asking about your name. And no, my mother didn't have cravings for peregrine falcons."

Basil started to laugh, and pain tore through him. He gasped and reached up, clutching at his chest. Lucian was there right away, fumbling to get a painkiller from his pocket. "Breathe," he ordered Basil.

Basil tried to obey, but it was hard.

He didn't feel like breathing. He didn't want to continue hurting this way. He wanted the pain to end, one way or another.

"We should find a hotel," Owen said.

Lucian nodded and helped Basil to his feet. The pain was still there, a strong ache in the center of Basil's chest.

Sometimes Basil had to resist the urge to look down and make sure someone wasn't tearing his chest apart.

"Wait," Peregrine said.

Lucian huffed. "What is it? What do you want from us? You saw what just happened. We need to get Basil somewhere he can rest."

Peregrine looked around instead of answering. Then, he turned his attention back to Basil. "Are you guys shifters?"

Lucian sucked in a breath. He'd started to think that Peregrine was strange and that his presence couldn't be a coincidence a few minutes earlier, and now he was sure of it. He didn't want to allow himself to hope, just in case, but he also couldn't ignore this.

"What do you know about shifters?" he asked.

Peregrine shrugged. "A lot, considering I'm one. So? Are you?"

"We are," Lucian confirmed.

"All four of you?"

Lucian wanted to grab Peregrine and shake him so he would get to the point, but he suspected Peregrine wouldn't take it well. "All four of us."

Peregrine slowly nodded. "And why are you in the city?"

"To find a healer."

"How is that going?"

Lucian was going to strangle the man if he didn't stop with the useless questions he already knew the answer to. "Not good," he said through gritted teeth. "If you're done, I need to get Basil to a safe place where he can rest. Unless you have information for us? Do you know where we can find a healer?"

Peregrine stared at him for a moment, and Lucian expected more questions. Instead, Peregrine turned his attention to

Basil. "You want to be healed."

Basil didn't roll his eyes, but Lucian did.

"Of course I do," Basil said.

"Why?"

Basil's eyes widened. "Because I don't want to die. I don't think anyone does."

"Why do you think you can find a healer here?"

Lucian and Lennox looked at each other. Lucian didn't know whether this guy was the shifter they were looking for or not, but there was a good possibility that if he wasn't, he knew where to find the caladrius. It was obvious that he was poking around and trying to find out whether or not they were dangerous, and if they wanted answers and help, they would have to play the game. It was dangerous, but they were in the middle of the city, surrounded by humans. Surely, even if this guy was a shifter, he wouldn't attack them or shift where everyone could see him.

They had to take that chance, unfortunately.

"My grandfather sent us," Lucian said.

That got Peregrine's attention. "Why?"

"He's a dire wolf shifter."

Peregrine didn't seem surprised or shocked. He cocked his head, very much like the pigeon Lucian had noticed earlier. "And?"

"Dire wolves are rare, and he's part of a rare shifter network. They help each other, keep each other safe, things like that. When we couldn't do anything for Basil, he reached out to that network. He knew of a kind of shifter who might be able to help, and while he wasn't able to contact the shifter directly, he found out that person was in the area. That's why we're here. To find him."

"And you think he's going to help you?"

"We have no way to know whether or not he will. The only way to find out is to find him, which is what we've been trying to do."

"Didn't have a lot of luck, though."

Lucian *was* going to strangle him if he continued like this. "Not yet. We'll find him, though." He tried to sound more confident than he felt.

"Basil doesn't have a lot of time left."

"We're all aware of that," Lennox intervened. "It's why we decided he should come with us rather than stay back home. Now, unless you know something, we should go. As you can see, Basil needs rest and peace."

Peregrine looked at Basil again. His expression didn't change, but eventually, he nodded. "Follow me," he said.

He turned around and walked away without waiting for them to say anything. Lucian looked at his brother and Lennox, wondering what they were supposed to do.

"I think we should follow him," Lennox said.

"Are you sure?" Owen asked. "He could be a serial killer."

"He could also know where the caladrius shifter is. We can't afford *not* to follow him." Lennox looked at Basil. "I can carry you if you don't think you can walk."

Lucian wasn't offended by the offer. He could carry Basil, too, but not as long as Lennox could. He wasn't as strong.

"I can walk," Basil said.

He wouldn't be doing it alone, and Lucian made sure Basil knew he could lean on him. He wrapped his arm around his mate's waist, allowing Basil to shift his weight. Then, the four of them followed Peregrine.

Luckily, he'd realized they weren't following, and he'd stopped. He was tapping his foot as he waited, and he kept looking around as if he expected something to happen. It made Lucian suspicious, and it also made him hope.

Could Peregrine be the caladrius shifter? Was that why he looked so anxious? If he *was* the caladrius shifter, he probably didn't want to stay in an open place for too long. It would make sense, but Lucian was terrified. What if he allowed himself to hope, only for that hope to be thwarted?

They followed Peregrine, and Lucian was surprised when he noticed they were headed back into the building they'd just left. He and Owen exchanged a glance, and Owen shrugged. He didn't have any more clues as to what was happening than Lucian did.

"I'll defend you if something happens," Lennox murmured. "You know what I can do. Make sure to stay behind me."

"I'll take care of Basil if that's the case. You focus on whatever the threat is," Lucian told him.

Lennox nodded. He didn't even look back at Lucian, but it was okay. Lucian felt better now that they had a plan. He hoped they wouldn't need it, but they didn't know if they could trust Peregrine. They didn't even know for sure that he was a shifter. Lucian suspected he was, since he'd known about them, but he could be wrong, and they might be in trouble.

They walked back into the building, and Peregrine headed for the stairs. He seemed to realize Basil wouldn't be able to climb them, and he corrected his direction, going for the elevator instead. He was still silent, and even though Lucian wanted nothing more than to demand answers, he kept his mouth shut. If Peregrine was the caladrius shifter, he might get offended and refuse to help. They needed to keep him happy, at least until they knew what was going on.

The five of them climbed into the elevator, but it was a tight fit. Peregrine grimaced and pressed his back against the wall, but he didn't protest. Lucian held Basil as close as he could, leaning down and murmuring to him, "What do you think?"

Basil shrugged. "He could be the shifter we're looking for, or he could be a serial killer. I don't know."

"Let's hope for the first one."

Basil grinned. "If it's the second one, feel free to leave me there and run."

Lucian knew he was trying to joke around, but he wasn't amused. "I'm not leaving you behind."

Basil's expression softened. "I know."

Lucian leaned down to kiss him. He kept it quick, mostly because he didn't trust Peregrine and wasn't sure what to make of him, and sure enough, when he looked up, Peregrine was staring at them. He snapped his gaze away, but Lucian had noticed.

The elevator finally stopped on the fifth floor. Peregrine wiggled out, and they all followed him to a door down the hallway. He unlocked it and scuttled in, leaving the door open for them.

Owen was the last one to enter, and he closed the door behind them.

The apartment was dark. Lucian looked around, but there wasn't much to see. Then a light came on, and he moved toward it. The room he walked into was a living room. It was small and only held a couch and a TV. Peregrine had settled on the couch and was staring at them.

"What now?" Owen asked, still looking around. He was tense.

Even though Owen wasn't a fighter, Lucian knew he wouldn't hesitate to throw himself into a fight to defend Basil. It made him happy to have found his brother again. He would have loved Owen even if he hadn't been ready for this, but it showed just how much Owen cared about him and Basil both.

Peregrine looked at Basil. "Now, you strip."

CHAPTER SIX

Basil didn't know what to do or say. Had Peregrine really just asked him to strip? And without telling him why he wanted him to?

"He's not going to strip for you," Lucian intervened.

Peregrine crossed his arms over his chest. "Doesn't he want to be healed?"

"He does. You can't just demand he do that without explaining why you want it, though."

Peregrine arched a brow. "Since I'm the one who will do the healing, I think I can demand anything I want."

Lucian opened his mouth, but Basil put a hand on his arm and squeezed. Lucian turned his attention to him, and Basil shook his head. "Let him be," Basil murmured.

"He just asked you to strip. You don't know why he wants that."

"Because he wants to heal me." Basil looked at Peregrine. "You're a caladrius shifter, aren't you?"

Peregrine stared at him for a moment before nodding. "I am. I have questions about how you found me, but they'll have to wait. This is more important."

"You're going to help me?"

"I will."

"Why? You don't know me."

Peregrine shrugged. "I don't have to give you an answer. I just need you to strip, at the very least, your chest. It's that, or you know where the door is."

Basil wasn't looking forward to stripping in front of a

stranger, or even Owen and Lennox, but he doubted there was a way out of it. Peregrine wasn't going to explain why he wanted Basil half-naked, but it seemed like he needed it to happen, and Basil wasn't going to protest. If this was the only way for him to be healed, it was a low price to pay.

"How should I pay you for this?" he asked as he took his jacket off.

"Not with money, if that's what you're asking."

"With what, then?"

"We can talk about it once I find out what's wrong with you. I'm not going to heal you right now. I just want to know what's going on. Once I know, I'll be able to tell how hard it'll be for me to heal you. Then, we can talk about payment."

Basil swallowed and nodded. He wanted to push, but once again, he didn't think he could. Peregrine had all the power in the situation, no matter how little Basil liked it. This was his only chance. They already knew that unicorn shifters couldn't help him, and it was a miracle they'd been able to find Peregrine. Basil wasn't going to put a stop to this, even if Peregrine tried to hurt him.

It wasn't like he had a long time to live anyway.

He handed his jacket to Owen, who took it and hugged it close. Basil did his best not to look at the others because he knew he would see his wariness and fear reflected in their expression. The only one who didn't look like that was Lennox, and he smiled at Basil when Basil held out his sweater. Owen took that, too, and bundled it in his arms.

Basil only had his t-shirt left, but Lucian grabbed his wrist before he could take it off. He pulled him close, kissing his forehead. "Are you sure about this?" he asked in a whisper.

"We don't have a choice. I have to do it, whether or not I'm sure."

"We'll have your back."

"I know you will. I trust you, just like I trust Owen and

Lennox. I wouldn't be here with you if I didn't."

"Once this is over, we're going on a trip. I don't care where or why, but I want some time alone with you."

"I'm not going to say no to that." Basil prayed he would have the opportunity to do it.

He took off his t-shirt, and this time, Lucian grabbed it. He nodded at Basil, who smiled at him and turned his attention back to Peregrine.

He wasn't surprised to see Peregrine watching him and Lucian. He seemed curious, but thankfully, he didn't ask whatever was on his mind. "Your jeans, too," he said instead.

Basil blinked. "You said I had to be bare-chested."

"It could work, but it would be better if you were in your underwear or naked. I'm pretty sure your boyfriend is going to kill me if I try to get you to take off your boxers, though, but the jeans have to go."

Basil sighed, but he obeyed.

The apartment was cold, and once he was standing in just his underwear and socks, he rubbed his arms. His skin had goosebumps, and he shivered.

"Good," Peregrine said as he got to his feet. "Lucian, you need to take a step back," he said.

Lucian wanted to say no. Basil could see it, and even though he loved his mate for doing this, they both knew he had to obey. Basil smiled at him, hoping to convince him. "I'll be fine," he said.

Lucian didn't look convinced, but he obeyed. He took a step back like Peregrine asked, but he hovered close.

Peregrine stopped in front of Basil. He winked at him, startling Basil. "You're hot, but you're not my type," he said.

Then, he shifted. His clothes dropped on the floor.

"I'm pretty sure that's the pigeon I noticed earlier," Lucian muttered.

Basil didn't answer, but he suspected his mate was right.

He'd noticed this pigeon earlier. Peregrine was a small bird, and he did look like a pigeon. He was white, and when Basil reached out to touch him, he flew away. Basil took it as an indication that he needed to be still, and he did his best to obey, even though he was cold.

Peregrine landed on Basil's shoulder. Basil felt him pull on his hair, and he bit his lower lip. It didn't hurt, but he needed to do *something*, and he couldn't.

Peregrine fluttered around Basil several times, going up and down, landing on his shoulders or on his arm when Basil held it out. Basil had no idea what he was doing, but he didn't feel any different. The pain was still there, a dull ache in his chest that became stronger every time he moved. He'd just taken a painkiller, so he would be good for at least a few hours, hopefully more. The painkillers didn't take away all the pain, though, and he still had to carry it.

Eventually, Peregrine landed in front of Basil. He shifted back, and once he was in his human form, he stared at Basil. He didn't seem to care that he was naked. He also didn't seem to be cold.

"Can he get dressed?" Lucian asked.

"It would be better if he didn't."

Instead of handing him his t-shirt, Lucian wrapped his arm around Basil's shoulders and held him close. Lucian was warm, and Basil curled against him without looking away from Peregrine.

Peregrine was still watching him. "Tell me about your parents," he said.

Basil frowned. "Why do you need to know about them?"

"Because I have a pretty good idea of what's going on with you, and I need to be sure before I do anything. What kind of shifter is your mother?"

Basil hesitated. He'd spent so long keeping that a secret that it felt weird to say it out loud. He already had, though, and this situation wasn't any different. Just like he'd trusted Lucian and his friends, he had to trust Peregrine. "She's a gorgon."

Peregrine nodded. "And you're a boy."

Basil's cheeks heated. He resisted the urge to hide his groin with his hands. "I am."

"What about your father?"

"He's a normal wolf shifter."

"I see. Well, this wouldn't have been a problem if you'd been born a girl. Although, don't ask me why. I'm a healer, not a scientist."

"What do you mean?"

"You're a chimera."

Basil took a moment to think about the word. "I know what that means in theory, but I'm not sure how it applies to me."

"You know that a chimera is made up of several different animals, right?" Basil nodded. Peregrine continued, "That's what you are. You're made up of a gorgon and a wolf."

"I've never been able to shift into either, though."

"That's because they're at war inside you. They both want to be the strongest, which is why you're in pain and getting weaker. They're using your energy to fight against each other, and they're going to kill you eventually."

"You talk as if they're actual entities."

"They kind of are. You don't realize it, because you've never been able to shift."

"Can you help him?" Lucian asked, impatient.

Peregrine stared at Basil for a while longer before nodding. "I think I can, yes."

Lucian didn't know what he thought of Peregrine, but as long as the shifter helped Basil, Lucian didn't care. He had no idea what Peregrine was thinking about or if he truly would be able to help Basil, but he was their last hope.

He looked at Owen and Lennox, trying to gauge their reaction. Owen looked entirely lost, while Lennox looked calm and serious like he always did. On the other hand, Basil looked hopeful, and Lucian hoped his heart wasn't about to be broken.

"It's fascinating, really," Peregrine continued. "Not only the fact that you're a male when you should have been female, but also how things went wrong and not only are you the wrong sex, but your gorgon and wolf parts are warring inside of you. I've never seen a case quite like yours."

"He's not a circus phenomenon," Lucian snapped.

Peregrine didn't look offended. If anything, he looked amused. "I'm very much aware of that. A lot of people find me fascinating, too. It doesn't mean I'm a monster or anything like that. It's just interesting."

"It's heartbreaking. He's dying. He's in pain. If you can help, please do. If you can't and just want to study him, tell us, and we'll go."

Peregrine shook his head. "I'm his only hope. And I *can* help him. There are a few decisions to make first, though." He looked at Basil again, dismissing Lucian. "I can get rid of one, but it's dangerous, and it could take part of you with it."

"What do you mean?" Basil asked.

Lucian wanted to rush, but he was grateful Basil was more levelheaded. It sounded like even though this option was possible, it wasn't safe, and they had to take into consideration everything before agreeing to whatever Peregrine was offering.

"Well, you're both gorgon and wolf shifter. There's no denying that. It's part of your nature, of yourself. If I get rid of one, it could take a part of your personality with it as it dies. I wouldn't recommend it, but it's an option, and you should know about it."

"What do you recommend, then?"

"I can fuse them together and make you a true chimera."

"I thought I was already one, since I'm part gorgon and part wolf shifter."

"You are, yet you're not. You contain both of them, but they're not fused, which is why you're sick. The better option here would be the second one. I can't tell you what your shifted form will end up being like, but you'd only have one, because they would be one, too."

"What's the downside of this option?"

Lucian almost smiled. Of course Basil had thought about this, too.

"You could die."

Lucian stared at Peregrine. Was he really that emotionless? Or was he just faking because he wanted to do this? He sounded fascinated by Basil, and he probably wanted to get his hands on him. He also wanted payment, which wasn't surprising. Lucian had no idea what he was going to ask, but it wouldn't be money. He would ask for favors, maybe things they couldn't give him now.

"Since I'm already dying, I'll choose option number two," Basil said.

Lucian tightened his arms around him. "Are you sure you don't want to think about it?" he murmured.

Basil looked up at him. "I don't have to. There's no right answer, and I have to choose the less bad one."

"You wouldn't die with the first option."

"Peregrine hasn't mentioned I would, no, but would I still be myself if I lost part of me? I don't want that to happen. I want to be myself and be with you. I know it's a risk, but I'm ready to take it." He paused. "Will you try to stop me?"

Lucian was offended, but only slightly. Basil didn't know him well, and he didn't know Lucian would never do something like that. Hell, he was tempted to do just that. He didn't want Basil to die, but Basil wasn't wrong. Would he truly be Basil if he was missing part of himself? "I won't," Lucian promised. "This is your decision, and no matter how much I dislike it, I can't do anything about it."

"You won't be able to intervene once I start," Peregrine warned. "You have to be aware of that. If you try to do anything once I'm healing him, it can be disastrous, both for him and for me. You could kill him."

"I won't," Lucian said.

"He's probably going to scream. It's going to be more painful than it has been until now."

Lucian glared at Peregrine. "Are you done with the lesson? I already promised I wouldn't intervene. I'll have Lennox hold me down if I need to. This is Basil's decision, and the only way he can make it. He made his choice."

Peregrine watched Lucian. Lucian didn't know what to make of it. He didn't *have* to make anything of it right now. He was focused on Basil, as he should be.

Peregrine finally nodded. "All right. Do you two want a moment to talk before we do this?"

Lucian looked down. These might be the last moments he and Basil had. If everything went well, Basil would make it out of this alive and healed. If they didn't, he would die.

Lucian's instincts told him to take Basil far away from Peregrine and make sure they never saw the man again. He couldn't do that, though. Taking Basil away would effectively kill him when he had a chance at living if he stayed, but it wasn't just that. Basil might be Lucian's mate, but Lucian couldn't make decisions for him. If Basil wanted to do this, Lucian had to be supportive.

Even if it broke his heart.

He understood there was no good answer in this situation. Basil was doing the best with what he had. Lucian understood why Basil had chosen the second option. If he'd been in Basil's place, he probably would have, too. There was no way to know what part of Basil would be lost if they went with that the first option, and Lucian couldn't imagine parting with his dire wolf. It wouldn't be the same, since Basil hadn't been aware of the gorgon and wolf inside him, but still. Having Peregrine get rid of one of them would take part of Basil with it, and that wasn't right. No shifter should have to go through something like that.

Lucian tightened his hold around Basil and kissed his forehead. "I'm scared," he admitted.

Basil smiled. "I would be worried if you weren't. I'm scared, too, but this is it. Once it's over, I'll be healed, and we can be happy."

"I should be more supportive."

"I don't think anyone would be. I understand you're afraid, and I share those fears. I made my decision, though, and I need to do this before I change my mind."

Lucian nodded and kissed Basil. If this was going to be their last kiss, he wanted to take it. "I love you," he murmured.

Basil blinked. "We've only known each other for a few days."

Lucian grinned. "And you've already asked me to marry you."

Lucian heard someone suck in a breath, but he kept his attention on Basil, whose cheeks were now pink.

"I didn't," Basil said.

"You might not have been serious, or maybe you were. Either way, I love you, and I do want to marry you once this is over."

"It's too soon."

"Not if we don't care about it." Lucian kissed Basil again. "But before we get hitched, you need to be healed."

Basil stared at Lucian for a moment before nodding and

turning to Peregrine again. "I want to do it. The second option. I want to fuse the gorgon and the wolf together."

Basil had come to terms with death. He didn't want to die, but he'd accepted that he probably would. Peregrine was offering him a way out of it, and he was going to take it.

It was the only option he could choose. He couldn't bear the thought of living only half a life. Peregrine apparently wasn't sure what would happen if he tried to take away either the gorgon or the wolf, and Basil didn't want to find out. He couldn't even choose. What part of himself could he want to get rid of? If he had no other option, he would go with the wolf, since it came from his father, but no matter how he'd ended up being a wolf shifter, it didn't change the fact that it was what he was. He didn't want to be anything different. He also didn't want to be in pain and dying, though, which was what had made this decision hard.

But he'd made it.

Peregrine nodded. "All right. You should probably sit down, or even better, lay on your back while I do this. It's going to be painful. I'll have to force the wolf and the gorgon together, and they won't be happy."

"Even if I start screaming and begging, don't stop. I need you to do this. I need you to heal me."

"I won't stop," Peregrine nodded. "You know, I like you."

Basil blinked. "You do?"

"A lot. I wasn't sure in the beginning. A lot of people try to find me so I can help them, which is why I usually observe them in my caladrius form before I talk to them."

"So you *were* the pigeon."

Peregrine grinned. "I was. I wanted to listen to your conversation and decide whether or not I should help you. You're strong, much stronger than I thought. A lot of people come here and beg. They're ready to give me anything so I'll help them."

"We are, too," Lucian said.

Basil resisted the urge to elbow him. He knew Lucian was terrified, probably more than he was himself. He'd come to terms with his death, but Lucian hadn't. Basil had been in pain for a long time, and he'd known he would die for most of it. Lucian was still trying to wrap his mind around that, and even though this was Basil's only chance, it wasn't surprising that Lucian wanted him to say no.

"That's one of the things I like about Basil. He has friends. He has you. You love him, and you're ready to do anything to help him." Peregrine cleared his throat. "We should start. You don't have a lot of time or energy left, Basil. We should do it before you're too weak to tolerate the pain."

Lucian walked Basil to the couch, a hand on the small of his back. Basil was glad for his touch. It reminded him of why he was doing this, of why he was risking death. He wanted to be with Lucian, and he wanted to be himself when he did so.

"I'll make sure he doesn't intervene," Lennox told Peregrine.

"Thank you. It would be a disaster if he were to do that. I don't know how Basil is going to react to what I do, but there are usually screams and begging. It's the pain. Not a lot of people are able to stand it, even when they know it's to save their life." Peregrine moved closer to the couch.

After one last kiss, he helped Basil lie on the couch, and with one last touch to Basil's hand, Lucian stepped away.

Basil followed him with his gaze. He stayed where Basil could see him, thankfully, and Basil knew he wouldn't be able to look away.

If he died, he wanted Lucian to be the last thing he saw.

"I'm not making any promises," Peregrine murmured once he was next to Basil. "I'm going to do my best, but your wolf and gorgon are strong. They might resist, and if I can't fuse them, you *are* going to die."

Basil nodded. "Do your best. It's all I'm asking for." It was all he *could* ask for. Peregrine was his only hope, and if he couldn't do this, Basil was dead.

Peregrine shifted. Basil held his breath, not sure what to expect. He wasn't surprised when Peregrine landed on his chest.

He *was* surprised when Peregrine started to glow.

It was incredibly pretty. Peregrine was a white bird, and the glow made him even whiter. Basil didn't have a lot of time to watch him, though, because that was when the pain hit.

It felt like he was being torn apart and put back together at the same time. The wolf and the gorgon were obviously resisting, and Basil bit his lower lip so hard that he tasted blood. Peregrine had said he would scream, but he didn't want to. Lucian would freak out if he did.

He resisted as much as he could. Eventually, though, he did open his mouth to scream.

He'd never felt anything like this. It was the worst pain he'd ever gone through, and he tried to get away from it. He had to. He was going to die otherwise, and it wasn't what he'd wanted when he'd come here.

Cool hands grabbed his before he could try to get off the couch. He tried to look at whoever was holding him, but he couldn't seem to be able to open his eyes. He thrashed, trying to get Peregrine off his body, but the light weight on his chest didn't move.

Then everything stopped.

Basil froze. His cheeks were wet with tears, and his throat felt raw. He waited for more pain, and when it didn't come, he opened his eyes. He wouldn't have been able to do this if he'd been watching Lucian the entire time. Lucian looked like he was about to faint. Lennox was holding him up, and while both of them were pale, Lucian was extremely so. Basil saw his hand tremble as he brought it to his mouth.

Basil swallowed. It hurt, but that was just because he'd been screaming. All the pain in his chest was gone, and he didn't know whether or not it was a good thing.

He rolled his head and looked down at Peregrine. He was still sitting on Basil's chest, and he was looking at him. Basil opened his mouth to ask him if it was over, but Peregrine took flight before he could.

Basil watched him as he flew to the window. He hadn't noticed it before, but it was open, which explained why it was so cold here. Peregrine flew through it and disappeared into the sky. Basil continued staring. He didn't know what he was supposed to do.

"Can I touch you now?" Lucian asked.

Basil didn't know. He started sitting up, and the same hands from before moved to help him. He realized it was Owen, and he smiled at him. "Thank you," he murmured. He grimaced at the pain in his throat.

"You're still in pain," Lucian said, sounding frantic. "It didn't work."

"I don't know if it worked, but I'm in pain because of the screaming. My chest feels fine." It felt more than fine — better than it ever had in Basil's life, which was both understandable and puzzling.

Basil had never known his body was a battle ground for a gorgon and a wolf. He'd always felt odd, but it had been normal to him. Now there was peace in his body. He felt normal, except for the fact that he was cold.

"Here," Owen said, handing Basil his sweater.

Lennox finally let go of Lucian, who rushed toward Basil and knelt by the couch. He took Basil's hands before Basil could take the sweater and squeezed them. "How are you feeling? Did it work?

"I think so."

Lucian looked around. Within a few seconds, he'd gathered Basil's clothes. Basil hoped Peregrine wouldn't mind. He didn't like being mostly naked in a place he didn't know. If Peregrine wasn't done, well, Basil would strip again. In the meantime, he'd feel better.

He didn't have the time to dress before Peregrine was back. He flew through the open window and landed in the middle of the room. Basil stared at him, wondering what was next.

Lucian couldn't deny Peregrine seemed to have done the job they'd wanted him to do. He wanted to strangle the man for the way he'd behaved, but the important thing was that Basil was fine.

Peregrine shifted. He eyed Basil, who was now sitting on the couch. He was much paler than before, and his knees didn't seem to be able to hold him up quite as well as they had. "How are you feeling?"

"Cold. I have a bit of a headache. It's nothing like the pain I went through before, though."

Peregrine nodded. "It's what I expected. You're healed."

"Can you tell me what it means? You said you were going to fuse the wolf and gorgon, but you never went into details."

Peregrine never got to the opportunity to answer. Before he could, the front door burst open. Peregrine squeaked and shifted, headed to the window, but a big owl came through it. It landed in the living room and shifted into a tall man who reached for Peregrine.

Peregrine managed to avoid him and made a beeline for Lucian. Lucian had no idea what was going on, but he didn't protest when Peregrine landed on his shoulder.

"Give him to us," one of the two men who'd burst in through the door said.

"Who are you?" Lucian asked. He put himself between Basil and the man. He'd just gotten his mate back from certain death. He wasn't going to risk him so soon after.

"None of your business. Give us the caladrius, and we'll let you go."

"If we don't?" Lennox asked. He sounded calm.

Lucian wondered if he actually was, or if he was freaking out on the inside like Lucian was.

"If you don't, you'll die, and we'll take him either way."

Lennox smiled and held out his hands. Peregrine squeaked on Lucian's shoulder, and Lucian reached up, catching him with his hands. He pulled Peregrine down so he could look him in the eyes. "Don't start freaking out. I'm going to stuff you into my jacket. That way, they can't snatch you. You'll be as safe as possible down there. We're going to do everything we can to get you out of here."

Peregrine nodded frantically, and Lucian did exactly what he'd said. He opened his jacket, stuffed the bird inside, and closed it again. Peregrine might still manage to sneak out from the bottom of the jacket, but he would be mostly safe. Who knew what would happen to him if he flew out the window? There could be other bird shifters out there waiting for him, and even though Lucian wasn't sure whether or not he liked him, he wasn't going to allow him to be caught.

Flames burst from both of Lennox's hands. Lucian was fascinated, at least until something behind him moved. Before he could turn to tell Basil to stay put, a huge dark form flew by him and landed square in front of him, Lennox, and Owen.

It could only be Basil, but Lucian couldn't believe his eyes. It was a wolf shifter, but it was much bigger than any other wolf shifters Lucian had ever encountered. That wasn't the only strange thing, either. Lucian would have to get a better look, but he was pretty sure his mate's fur was made of scales rather than hair. It was black, and every time he moved, it glittered in the light.

"What the fuck is that?" one of the men who'd come in through the door asked.

Basil roared. Lucian noticed his tongue was forked, but that was all he had the time to notice before Basil threw himself at the two men.

Lucian wanted to help him, but he didn't have to. Basil got rid of them in seconds. The first man fell, and he never got up. The second one took a look around, noticed that Lennox was burning the third guy to a crisp, and turned around to flee. Lucian stayed tense, wondering if anyone else was going to come in. When no one did, Owen strode to the front door and slammed it closed. He leaned against it, his eyes wide, and looked around.

Lucian did the same. Lennox was standing by the window. A small amount of ashes and burning coals was at his feet, and he frowned down at it. The air smelled of burning meat. It turned Lucian's stomach.

Basil was still standing in the middle of the living room in his shifted form. Lucian took a step toward him, and Basil sat, cocking his head. It was almost as if he wondered whether Lucian was afraid of him, and Lucian wanted him to know that wasn't the case.

He crouched in front of Basil and reached for him. Basil stayed still as Lucian touched him, and he smiled when he realized he was right. Basil didn't have fur. His entire body was covered in scales like a serpent's. It was odd but gorgeous, and Lucian was surprised when he felt Basil's skin was warm. For whatever reason, he'd always expected snakes to be cold, but Basil wasn't.

"You're beautiful," Lucian murmured.

Basil grinned, exposing his fangs and his forked tongue. It flickered, and Basil's eyes widened. He probably hadn't expected whatever sensation the tongue gave him.

Something squirmed against Lucian's chest, and he remembered Peregrine. He got to his feet and opened his jacket. Peregrine peeked out. When he saw no one else was there, he flew out and landed next to Basil. He shifted, all his attention on Basil.

"You're gorgeous," he said. "You're one of my best works. The gorgon and the wolf truly meshed together well."

Lennox cleared his throat. "Basil, why don't you shift back? I think Peregrine should tell us about the men who attacked, and it would be better if you were in your human form. The two of you should get dressed."

Peregrine looked like he wanted to protest, but one glare from Lucian made him move toward his clothes. Basil seemed to have a harder time shifting back into his human form, so Lucian went to stand next to him and talked him through it. It had to be strange to shift for the first time in your twenties. Lucian couldn't imagine how it felt, but if his mate needed help with the shift, he was more than happy to be there for him.

As soon as Basil was in his human form again, Lucian dragged him into his arms. "I thought I was going to lose you."

Basil hugged Lucian back. "You didn't, though. I'm sorry you had to go through this."

Lucian snorted. "You were the one who had to go through it, not me."

"But you had to hear me scream. I can only imagine how hard it was."

"Basil?" Lennox asked. "Here are your clothes."

Lucian leaned away from his mate and kissed him. "We'll have time to talk later. Right now, I think we should leave this place as soon as possible."

Basil nodded, and this time, he managed to get his clothes on. Once he was dressed, they all turned their attention to

Peregrine. Thankfully, he was dressed, too, and he was scowling.

"What happened?" Lennox asked.

"That's what I was talking about when you mentioned payment. I want help."

"What kind of help?" Lucian asked.

Peregrine's shoulders slumped, and he suddenly looked much older than he had until now. "You don't have any idea of what my life is like." He paused and looked at Lennox. "Although maybe you do. You're a phoenix shifter, aren't you?"

"I am. Those men were here to take you away."

"As you can imagine, a lot of people want my power. I've been hiding all my life. Sometimes, people manage to find me, usually after I heal someone. That's probably how those three guys found me."

"Because you healed me?" Basil asked.

"No. That was too recent. But you're not the only person I've healed, and obviously, someone told these guys about me and where to find me. It's been like this all my life. I have to keep running, keep hiding, and always look behind myself. I want it to stop."

Lucian frowned. "I don't know if we can do that."

"You could come back with us to Rosewood," Owen intervened, glaring at Lucian.

Lucian hadn't meant anything bad with his words. He wanted to help Peregrine, not just because Peregrine had saved Basil, but also because no one should live the way he had been. Lucian wasn't sure there was anything they could do, though. They couldn't exactly go after every single person who might want to get their hands on Peregrine, and they couldn't play bodyguard for the rest of his life.

"Rosewood?" Peregrine asked.

"It's a pack. Initially, they were all wolf shifters, but they welcomed several kinds of rare shifters. All of us live there in peace, and we're protected."

Peregrine's eyes were narrow. "What kind of shifters?"

"Well, you know my mate is a phoenix shifter. I'm a dire wolf. There are two unicorn shifters there, too, and a jackalope, as well as Lennox's twin."

"And you're not prisoners?"

"We're not. One of the unicorn shifters is mated to the alpha. They're together, and they're happy. I can promise you no one is going to hurt you if you agree to come with us, and I think it's your best chance."

Peregrine looked at the window again, then, at the pile of ash under it. "I suppose it's not like I have a choice. I have to move again anyway, so I might as well go to Rosewood." He looked at Owen again. "When do we leave?"

CHAPTER SEVEN

By the time the five of them got to Rosewood, they were exhausted. Basil wanted nothing more than to find his bed and spend the next two days in it, but of course, it wasn't that easy. As soon as Lennox parked the car in front of Camden's house, the front door flew open and people rushed out.

Basil's mother was at the front, and she opened the back door before Basil could, pushing herself inside and hugging him. "I knew you could do it!"

Peregrine cleared his throat. "If anything, I'm the one who did it," he pointed out.

Basil laughed and hugged his mom. "Mom, this is Peregrine, and like he said, he's the one who healed me. Peregrine, this is my mom."

"The gorgon. It's a pleasure to meet you."

It took Basil a few moments to untangle himself from his mom, and by the time he did, everyone else was out of the car. Peregrine's stance was stiff as he looked around, maybe to find the rare shifters prisoner or something like that. Basil had done pretty much the same thing when he'd first arrived. Both he and Peregrine had been on the run all their lives, and it was hard to believe that Rosewood truly was a safe place for shifters like them.

"Welcome to Rosewood," Camden said. He kept his distance from Peregrine, no doubt noticing how tense the caladrius shifter was.

Peregrine nodded at him. "Thank you for allowing me to come. Has Lennox told you why I'm here?"

"Because you're hunted. You're not the only one, so you don't have to worry about that. The pack will keep you as safe as possible."

"And you won't try to force me to heal anyone?"

"No. I'm sure both our healer and my mate and his brother will be eager to talk to you, but no one will force you to do anything. You're free to leave or stay. If you decide to stay, you can have a room in the alpha house, at least until you want your own place. If you'd rather have a place from the beginning, we can work something out. As you can see, we have a limited number of houses."

Peregrine looked around again. "I do see. It's pretty."

Camden smiled. "And safe. I won't lie to you. Some people know about Toby and Sam, and others about Lennox and Casey. Their presence here isn't a secret, and I'm sure that eventually, people will find out about you. The fact that Rosewood is a safe place for rare shifters is making the rounds, so some things will have to change here. You're welcome to become a pack member, though, or you can stay until you get your legs under you and leave once you have."

Peregrine looked lost, but he slowly nodded. "Thank you. I think I'll take advantage of that for at least a while."

"Good." Camden looked at Basil. "I'm happy to see you're feeling better."

"It's all thanks to Peregrine."

"Which is one of the reasons he's welcome here with the pack. Why don't you come in, Peregrine? You can choose a room, and we can talk about any doubts you might have about staying with us. Basil, you look about to drop. You're still in the same bedroom, and I'm sure Lucian and you won't mind sharing."

Basil didn't feel that tired suddenly. He'd been exhausted, mostly because they'd decided to drive as quickly as they'd driven toward Peregrine, just in case anyone was following him. They hadn't had any problem, but now they all needed rest.

This would be the first time Basil and Lucian shared a bed when he was feeling okay, though. Lucian had stayed with him when he was sick, either cuddling with him on the bed or sitting in the chair next to him. They hadn't done much more than kiss, and Basil had yearned for more.

He still did. Now, he had the opportunity to make that happen. He wasn't in pain anymore. He felt good, even though he was still puzzled. He knew his life had changed for the better, and he wanted to explore everything his shifted form could do, but not right now.

Right now, he wanted to explore Lucian.

"You have to tell me everything," Basil's mom said.

Basil smiled at her. "And I will, as soon as I get some sleep. I promise I'm fine, and you're going to be amazed at what Peregrine managed to do. I really do need rest, though."

His mom arched a brow, clearly not fooled. "Fine. But I'll be in the living room when you wake up. I want to hear everything that happened."

"Just like everyone else."

Luckily for Basil and Lucian, no one tried to stop them after that. They could see how frantic Basil was to get Lucian alone, if the little smiles on their faces were anything to go by. Basil didn't care that he was transparent. He only cared about getting Lucian into bed.

He burst out laughing when he got to the bedroom he'd occupied before and saw a bottle of lube on the nightstand. "Who do you think left it there?" he asked Lucian.

Lucian grinned. "Probably Toby. I'm ready to bet he came in here to leave it there as soon as Owen called him to tell him everything went fine."

Basil locked the door behind them and reached for his jacket. "Well, I'm going to have to thank him once we're done here."

He took his jacket off and threw it on top of the dresser. He didn't waste time, taking off his t-shirt, his shoes, and his socks before noticing Lucian wasn't stripping.

Basil hadn't even asked him what he wanted, had he? "We don't have to do anything if you're not feeling up to it, or if it makes you uncomfortable," he said. "We can just get into bed and sleep."

Lucian's smile was soft. "That's not the problem. It's just incredible to see you healthy."

"You can also feel me being healthy." Basil wiggled his eyebrows. "Not to push you or anything, but I wouldn't mind if you were ready for more than kissing."

Lucian snatched him around the waist and pulled him closer. "I'm more than ready, as long as you are."

"I've been ready since the first time I saw you."

"You were almost unconscious."

Basil reached around Lucian and squeezed one of his ass cheeks. "You know what I mean. I wanted you when I thought I was going to die, and I want you now, too. I want us to start our life together. We had to wait because of how sick I was, but I'm not anymore. We can be together now." And forever, although Basil didn't add that bit.

Lucian had teased him about getting married a few times, and while Basil had brushed him off, he hadn't been able to stop thinking about it. He hoped it would be in their future, but for now, the only thing he could focus on was the bed and what they'd be doing in it.

Lucian kissed him, and Basil melted against him. He didn't care what they did, just that they finally got time in bed that wasn't dedicated to sleeping. They didn't even have to use the lube Toby had left on the nightstand. Basil was up for any-thing—quite literally at this point—even if it was frotting or rutting against each other like teenagers.

They staggered toward the bed, not letting go of each other. Basil had a hard time thinking. The only thing he wanted was to get Lucian naked, and he wanted it now.

They stumbled over Basil's shoes, almost missing the bed. Lucian swore when he fell backward, but luckily for them, they were close enough that even though Lucian was too much on the right, he didn't fall on his face, taking Basil with him. Instead, he ended up half-hanging off the bed, and Basil laughed as he rolled to his back to give his mate space to right himself.

Since they weren't plastered against each other anymore, Basil quickly unbuttoned his jeans and pushed them down his legs. "We should probably grab a shower," he said. He was still wearing the same clothes he'd had on when Peregrine had healed him.

Lucian knee-walked until he was on all fours on top of Basil. "We can do that, or we can do it after we get some rest."

"We both know we're not going to rest right now."

"We could."

Basil scowled. "Don't you even try. I want you naked, dammit. I don't care if you stink." Basil paused. "Although I'll pass on blowing you until we can clean up."

Lucian laughed and kissed the tip of Basil's nose. "Fine. Both mouths stay above the shoulders. It's not like we can't come up with something fun to do even that way."

Basil pushed Lucian away. "Exactly. Now, get naked."

Basil was happy when Lucian finally obeyed. He stared, not one bit ashamed of it. Lucian was his mate, and he was *hot*.

His limbs were long and lean, with obvious muscle, but not too much of it. He was hairy, something that thrilled Basil, but his groin was neatly trimmed. Basil even loved the slight pouch on Lucian's stomach. It made him seem more human but just as perfect in Basil's eyes.

115

"You're looking at me like you want to eat me," Lucian said as he stood there.

He was hard, and Basil allowed his gaze to linger. He was going to have fun. "Maybe I do."

"We just said no mouths below the shoulders."

"Fine. I'll keep that for dessert after we sleep and shower, then." Basil opened his arms. "Come here."

He was relieved he didn't have to ask twice. Lucian crawled back onto the bed. He stopped on his way to Basil, hooking his fingers under the elastic band of Basil's underwear and pulling them down. Basil wiggled to help, grinning when Lucian threw the underwear behind himself and finally lowered on top of Basil.

Basil hooked his ankles around Lucian's legs and pushed his hips up. The contact was maddening, making him feel both like he wanted more and like he was about to explode if he got it, especially when Lucian thrust down at the same time. Basil moaned loudly, something that seemed to amuse Lucian if his smile was anything to go by. He silenced Basil with a kiss. Basil was grateful for it because Lucian kept grinding against him, making him moan and groan even louder.

"I thought I was going to lose you," Lucian murmured against Basil's lips. "I don't know what I would have done if Peregrine hadn't been able to help."

"You'll never have to find out. I'm not going anywhere. You're stuck with me."

Lucian's eyes shone. "Promise?"

"Promise." Basil's throat felt tight, and he was glad they stopped talking after that.

They chased their pleasure, and Basil wasn't surprised when Lucian made sure he had everything he needed. His mate always did. Lucian was a caretaker, and while it might be because Basil had been sick when they'd met, he hoped it would continue. He wanted Lucian to take care of him, and he wanted to take care of Lucian.

Lucian shuddered and buried his face against Basil's throat. Basil groaned when he felt the nip of teeth. He screwed his eyes shut and pushed up even harder, needing to come. The bite on his shoulder turned harder just as Lucian snaked a hand between their bodies and wrapped his fingers around both their cocks. It was a tight fit, but Basil didn't care because he was about to come.

He came first, biting on his lower lip so he wouldn't alert the entire house as to what they were doing. Lucian made a sound that was half chuckle and half moan as he continued jacking both of them off, using Basil's seed as lube. Basil shuddered, the sensations almost too much, but he didn't want to give up until Lucian came, too.

When he did, Basil kissed him and swallowed his moans. They kissed sloppily, both of them coming down from their pleasure high, until Lucian's weight became too much for Basil. He squirmed, looking down at his stomach when Lucian shifted off him. "We *really* need a shower now," he complained.

Lucian huffed and rolled, snatching his t-shirt from the floor. He used it to clean up Basil, then himself, before balling it up and throwing it down again. "There. Will that be enough until we wake up?"

Basil snuggled against Lucian's side. "Already thinking I'm too high maintenance?"

Lucian kissed Basil's forehead and gathered him into his arms. "Never. You're not high maintenance. You're just right for me."

And wasn't that the truth.

YOU MAY ALSO ENJOY THE FOLLOWING FROM EXTASY BOOKS INC:

Despised Fangs
Catherine Lievens

Excerpt

Darren stared at the door of his cell.

He was bored.

He didn't know how long he'd been locked up, but he supposed it didn't matter. It wasn't like he'd be let free anytime soon. He had a hard time getting used to it, though. He hated being locked up and having to look at the same four walls day after day, week after week.

But he was lucky. He didn't know what had happened to the other dhampirs he'd worked with before being captured, but he could imagine. They probably weren't in a nice cell the way he was. If they were lucky, their death had been fast.

The only reason Darren hadn't been killed was that he'd agreed to help the vampires. His father would kill him if he ever found out about this, so all in all, Darren didn't mind being stuck here that much. It was better than having to deal with his father, which was why he hadn't protested much the past few times Oren had visited him for information. He always made a point of bitching, but his heart wasn't in it.

If he was honest, the situation wasn't as bad as it could be. For one, he wasn't dead. The cell also wasn't what he'd imagined the vampires would stick him in if they ever caught him. He'd thought it would be small, dark, and damp. Instead, it was comfortable. The mattress was soft, as was the pillow. He had plenty of blankets, and he needed it since the cell was always cold. But he even had a TV and a small table with a chair where he ate his meals.

And they were good. He wasn't starving like he'd expected. He had no idea who cooked since vampires only drank blood, but whoever did was a good cook.

Darren had no idea how long he was going to be stuck here, and while he wasn't looking forward to it, it was better than the alternative. He was grateful that the vampires hadn't killed him. It would have turned him into a vampire, and while he'd realized that not all vampires were monsters like his father had always told him, he wasn't looking forward to an immortal life drinking blood and staying out of the sun.

He liked being tanned, thank you very much.

When he heard footsteps come closer, he sat up on his bed and stared at the cell door. It was too soon for his next meal, so it had to be something else. Did Oren need more information? Darren wouldn't be surprised. He knew what his father was planning, even though he hadn't told anyone about it. Dhampirs would continue arriving in town in waves, and they wouldn't leave, not alive. The problem was that killing them turned them into vampires, which was something no one wanted. Dhampirs were vampire hunters because of what they were, and vampires didn't want to create vampires who hated them and would have an easy time killing them once they were immortal.

A key slid into the lock, and the cell door creaked open. Darren peeked out, but it wasn't Oren. A guard stood there, peering in, and Darren grinned. He knew that some vampires, especially younger ones, were fascinated by him. He understood it. There weren't a lot of dhampirs around, and they were no doubt curious.

He raised his hand and wiggled his fingers. "You need me?" he asked.

The vampire straightened, and Darren was pretty sure he was blushing. He hadn't even realized it was possible. "There's someone here to see you."

"Oh? Who is it?"

"Falkner."

Darren grumbled, but he was secretly happy to see Falkner. "Do I really have to go?"

The guard looked nonplussed. "I suppose not, but I should let him know. Do you want to stay in your cell?"

This guard was no fun. Oren always snarked back, and he and Darren ended up bickering with each other. It gave Darren a distraction. "No." He got to his feet. "I'll come." If anything, it would distract him for a moment. He would be bored again soon enough.

Darren stretched, grinning when he saw the vampire was staring at him. He made a show out of it, even though he had no intention of doing anything more. He didn't know if the vampire was just fascinated with him or if there was something more there, but he wasn't about to have a relationship with anyone, let alone a vampire.

"Where to?" he asked as he stepped closer to the door.

"The interrogation room."

"You know, you guys really should have a room dedicated to this. Where do the other prisoners meet their families?"

"They don't."

Darren supposed that answered his question. "Why not?"

"Because they don't stay prisoners for long."

Because they died. He didn't have to say it for Darren to understand. "Is anyone planning on killing me?" He made sure to keep his voice light, even though he was tense. If something was going to happen to him, he wanted to know.

"Not as far as I know. Oren forbid anyone to touch you in any way."

"I knew he liked me."

"I think he likes the information you can give him more."

Darren huffed. "Way to break my heart."

The vampire stepped aside so Darren could move into the hallway. He didn't bother handcuffing Darren, but then, Darren couldn't go anywhere. There was no way for him to run, and even though he could attack the guard, it wouldn't be useful. He was just a human, and without weapons and help, he was useless against the vampire.

So Darren walked next to the guard, looking around and making the most out of the situation. He would be back in his cell soon enough, even though he wasn't looking forward to it.

The guard didn't come into the interrogation room with him. Instead, he opened the door and let Darren in before closing and locking it behind him.

Falkner was sitting at the table, and he smiled when he saw Darren. He got to his feet, maybe to hug Darren.

Darren was horrified at the thought. "What are you doing here?"

Falkner didn't look angry at Darren's harsh words. "I'm here to see you, of course."

"You shouldn't continue to come. It doesn't make sense for you to, and I can't imagine your boyfriends are happy about it. Who came with you today?"

"Andrew, and you're right. He wasn't happy. I won't stop coming, though."

"Why not?" Darren knew he was pushing too hard. He might have told Falkner to stay away, but he was secretly happy and incredulous, and he didn't want their friendship to stop. He didn't understand why Falkner was doing this, but if Falkner didn't come to visit, he would be alone most of the time. He still was, but he looked forward to the weekly visits from Falkner. Sometimes, he came even more often. It was a break from a boring routine, but it also made Darren feel like someone cared.

His father certainly wouldn't. He had to know what had happened to Darren, although maybe he didn't know that Darren was still alive. The other dhampirs wouldn't be, and that, he would be aware of. Darren didn't think his father would care even if he were dead, which was one of the reasons he was happy Falkner did.

Falkner didn't owe him anything. Darren owed him since he'd almost killed him, but instead of being angry and demanding Darren's head on a silver platter, Falkner visited him and acted as if they were friends. It didn't make sense, but Darren had stopped trying to understand what was going on in Falkner's mind.

"Because we're friends," Falkner said simply.

"I'm pretty sure friends don't try to kill each other."

Falkner smiled. "You didn't try to kill me, not really."

"All right. Then, I tried to use you to get to your coven."

"You did, but your heart wasn't in it."

Darren was mildly offended. "What are you talking about? Of course my heart was in it."

Falkner arched a brow, but he didn't call out Darren's lie. "Why don't you sit down?"

Darren huffed, but he obeyed. He was glad Falkner wasn't going anywhere, even though he didn't understand why.

About the Author

Catherine is the creator of several series, most of them paranormal, including the Whitedell Pride Series and the Gillham Pack Series. While she graduated in translation, she decided to go the writer's way because it was more fun to create her own stories and characters.

She's been living in Italy for more than twenty years, but she's a daughter of the North—Belgium to be precise—and she misses it so much that she's already planning to move back.

She loves pizza—probably too much—her son, her pets, and of course, books. She sneaks some reading time into her schedule every time she has five minutes free from writing, demands from her various pets and son, and lastly, housework.

Connect with her:

lievens.catherine@gmail.com
BookBub: https://www.bookbub.com/authors/catherine-lievens
Website: https://authorcatherinelievens.com/
Facebook: https://www.facebook.com/catherine.lievens.9
Facebook Group: https://www.facebook.com/groups/411788002341528/
Twitter: https://twitter.com/authorCLievens
Newsletter: http://eepurl.com/c-uvKn